SPOOKSMITHS INVESTIGATE
CIRCUS of SHADOWS

NECROPOLIS RAILWAY
ONE-WAY COFFIN TICKET
THIRD CLASS *Necropolis City*
WATERLOO TO ~~HOLLOW HILLS CEMETERY~~

To save your parents, whistle for the train.
I'm dying to put you to work.

*To Bill, Ellie and Edward,
thank you for believing in me.*

First published in the UK in 2025 by Usborne Publishing Limited., Usborne House, 83-85 Saffron Hill, London EC1N 8RT, England, usborne.com

Usborne Verlag, Usborne Publishing Ltd., Prüfeninger Str. 20, 93049 Regensburg, Deutschland, VK Nr. 17560

Text copyright © Alex Atkinson, 2025

The right of Alex Atkinson to be identified as the author of this work has been asserted by her in accordance with the Copyright, Designs and Patents Act, 1988.

Cover illustration by Miriam Serafin © Usborne Publishing Limited, 2025

The name Usborne and the Balloon logo are Trade Marks of Usborne Publishing Limited.

All rights reserved. No part of this publication may be reproduced or used in any manner for the purpose of training artificial intelligence technologies or systems (including for text or data mining), stored in retrieval systems or transmitted in any form or by any means without prior permission of the publisher.

This is a work of fiction. The characters, incidents, and dialogues are products of the author's imagination and are not to be construed as real. Any resemblance to actual events or persons, living or dead, is entirely coincidental.

A CIP catalogue record for this book is available from the British Library.

ISBN 9781835400999   9751/1   JFMAMJJ SOND/25

Printed and bound using 100% renewable electricity by CPI Group (UK) Ltd, CR0 4YY

SPOOKSMITHS INVESTIGATE
CIRCUS OF SHADOWS

ALEX ATKINSON

1

It's late afternoon on a cold October evening when the dead call. Rusty, my twin brother, and I are surrounded by empty crisp packets and huddled over our homework at the kitchen table. All is quiet until the landline rings.

Rusty slams down his pen. "Indigo, it's your turn."

I groan because he's right and there's no getting out of it. We both know whoever's calling won't stop until one of us picks up.

Grudgingly, I leave the bright and cosy kitchen and, less grudgingly, my maths homework, and go out into the darkening hallway. I walk slowly because I know this isn't a normal call.

The dead always ring when Mum and Dad aren't around. Dad's out at the coffin workshop (which comes with the territory when your family owns a funeral parlour) and Mum's on her counselling course.

These "special" phone calls have been coming for weeks; ever since Rusty and I discovered we're Spooksmiths and have the power to talk to ghosts; ever since we defeated the Cinderman, a Category Five monster ghost who tried to take over our town and turn everyone into zombies.

A grey shape flits across the mirror at the end of the corridor – a shape that looks like a veiled woman in a long dress. I quickly click the lamp on, creating a pool of light around me. The mirror shows only my own startled reflection framed by frizzy curls. Maybe I imagined it. I take a deep breath and pick up the still-ringing phone.

"Serenity Funerals," I say into the mouthpiece.

The connection flutters, like a trapped bird.

"Hello?"

Crackling static mixes with a frantic, distant whispering, like someone wants to get through but can't make themselves heard.

I know from the goosebumps rippling over my skin that the person on the other end of the phone isn't alive. Being a

Spooksmith is a supernatural ability that skips generations in our family and landed with me and my twin brother on our twelfth birthday. Officially, WORST. GIFT. EVER. I'm not sure either of us will ever get completely comfortable with it, but one of the hardest things is keeping it a secret from Mum and Dad. They're just plain old Smiths with no ghostly abilities whatsoever. Even though they work in a funeral parlour, finding out the world is haunted, and that their children speak "spook", might just blow their minds.

"If I can't hear you, I can't help you," I say, somehow managing to keep the wobble out of my voice.

There's a *click* and the line goes dead.

Although the goosebumps on my arms start to fade, my hands are shaking so much it takes me a few goes to put the phone back in its cradle.

"Let me guess," says Rusty, as I walk back into the kitchen. "You've just been ghosted."

I roll my eyes at his rubbish joke and grab another bag of cheesy crisps from the cupboard, more for a distraction than because I'm actually hungry.

"How bad was it?" asks Rusty, eyeing my tight grip on the cheesy crisps.

"I think they're getting angry that we can't understand them. I could sense it."

I sit down at the table, ripping open the packet and shoving a handful of crisps in my mouth. I wish, just once, we could be contacted by a ghost we want to hear from. Like Grandpa. He was the first ghost we met and the one who helped us understand our powers, but he disappeared when we defeated the Cinderman.

We don't know why some ghosts stick around and others move on. It seems to have something to do with feeling fulfilled. We think that's why Grandpa left – helping us set him free.

Unfortunately, not every ghost's idea of "fulfilled" comes from a happy, positive place. While Grandpa was a peaceful Category One ghost, the Cinderman was a Category Five, the type that wants to cover your hometown in ash and suck the life out of everyone you know.

We have urns full of the life-sucking variety of ghost trapped in a secret crypt beneath our house. How our ancestors trapped them, we don't know. All we do know is that it's a key part of a Spooksmith's job to keep them that way and stop them from terrorizing the living.

There's a squawk from outside followed by a stream of rude words. Phrank must be welcoming Dad home.

It's a long story, but to call Phrank "just a pheasant" would be really underselling his skills. He's my animal sidekick and the self-appointed guard pheasant of 33–34 Deadman's Drive. He also comes in handy in an evil ghost situation.

No one gets past Phrank. If he's not asleep.

As if on cue there's another loud squawk from the garden, followed by a clatter as the front door is thrown open.

"Hello?" calls Dad.

"We're in here," I call back.

Dad strides into the kitchen in his long black funeral coat. It really adds to his tall, thin and sombre vibe. All he needs is a pair of fingerless gloves and he'd look like a character from a Charles Dickens novel. He eyes the salty snacks on the table.

"You two were supposed to make pasta for dinner."

I'm about to argue that at least we're doing our homework, but before a row can get started, Phrank announces Mum's return from her counselling course with another flurry of carks.

"Ow!" shouts Mum, slamming the door shut. "That cheeky little so-and-so was trying to bite my hand!"

The Phrank of old – before the Spooksmith thing kicked off – would peck anyone in sight. Now he protects the house and the family, so why would he peck Mum?

My question is answered when Mum walks into the kitchen trailing a strange, smoky smell instead of her normal flowery perfume. I notice the smell is coming from a letter in her hand.

My Spooksmith senses are tingling and I sit up straighter. Phrank's highly attuned to spooky stuff. What if he was aiming for the letter, not Mum?

"They haven't eaten dinner." Dad looks at me and Rusty and tuts.

"But I left pasta…" says Mum, looking more annoyed by the second.

I'm not interested in dinner.

"Where did you get that?" I ask.

"It was in the letter box at the end of the drive. It's addressed to all of us." Before I can stop her, Mum rips open the envelope. Her eyebrows shoot up as she reads the card inside and then passes it to Dad.

"What is it?" I ask, craning my neck to try to read it.

"It's an invitation," he says, and places it on the table.

> THE COMPANY OF THE SMITH FAMILY IS DESIRED
> AT A GATHERING OF THE GUILD OF TRADITIONAL
> UNDERTAKERS
> FRIDAY 13TH OCTOBER
> FIVE O' CLOCK IN THE AFTERNOON
> 121 WESTMINSTER BRIDGE ROAD, LONDON

Dad does a little fist pump, but it's such an un-Dad move I'm not sure I believe my own eyes.

"And this is a good thing?" asks Rusty, wrinkling his nose at the smell and probably also at the thought of the most boring party on Earth.

"It's the Guild!" says Dad. "The oldest funeral organization in the world!" He's grinning like a kid at Christmas.

"I still feel like there's something I'm not getting…" says Rusty.

"Me too," I add.

"Only the best and most distinguished funeral homes are asked to join the Guild. It's a very prestigious and secretive body. I haven't heard it mentioned in years. I assumed it had been disbanded, but obviously not." Dad picks up the invitation, cradling it like it's made of gold.

"And that's not all," says Mum, producing several sets of tickets from the bottom of the envelope. "Look! Train tickets are included and free entrance to Clarence Caring's house!"

From the look of joy on Mum's face, this Clarence character must be some counselling guru who she idolizes, but I don't ask because I don't want a long lecture on his life and work.

"And—" Mum doesn't get to finish her sentence because Rusty is already squealing.

"Palladium Level Battle Beast Universe passes! I can access every exhibit!" He snatches the blood-red passes from Mum with a hungry grin. He'll never miss an opportunity to geek out on his obsession with that monster game. He's been trying to get our parents to take him to London to visit Battle Beast Universe for years.

I'm the only one not jumping for joy. Who is this strange smoky-smelling guild that thinks it can buy my family with a few free tickets?

I clear my throat. "Look, I don't want to poop on this party, but it's in four days' time. What about the funeral parlour? You always say it won't run itself."

"I can hire in help," says Dad.

Dad hasn't taken a day off in living memory. I can't believe I'm going to say this next part, but here goes...

"What about school?"

"Inset day!" Rusty yells gleefully.

I try again: "Don't you think this ancient guild popping up and buying you all your dream days out is just a bit...well, strange?"

"These might change your mind," says Mum. She smiles and hands me two *London Zoo, Keeper for the Day* passes from the envelope.

I bite my lip. I want to be a vet when I'm older. I'm not

a big fan of keeping animals in cages, but London Zoo is run by a conservation charity dedicated to helping species that are at risk of extinction. I've wanted to go since for ever, but Mum and Dad are always so busy and a trip to London is expensive...

I can't shake the feeling that something weird is going on, but there's no way I'm turning this opportunity down. So I say nothing else.

"Great," says Dad. "Everyone is on board. Let's book a hotel." And he sprints from the room to find the laptop with a manic gleam in his eyes.

He shouts from the office for Mum to dig out the credit card, so she's next to leave, closely followed by Rusty, who's chattering about some Battle Beast characters called the Miasmic Mawk and Harknock the Heinous.

Soon, I'm all alone in the kitchen.

I pick up the invitation. Brown blotches have bled onto the edges of the cream card and the black, spidery writing is dull. The smell of smoke clings to it like fleas to a fox. It reminds me of when the Cinderman covered Greyscar, our small seaside town, in ash...

No. I'm not going there. This is a good thing – a rare family outing that manages to please everyone. After everything we've been through, we all deserve some time off.

I put the invitation down and follow my family into the office, trying to ignore Phrank, who is sitting by the kitchen door squawking at me with a disapproving look in his eyes.

2

Friday rolls around quicker than a hedgehog into a ball. Instead of being stuck in school, I'm at London Zoo with Dad, fulfilling a lifelong dream and feeding a giant Galapagos tortoise prickly pears for lunch. Even Dad is looking interested. I mean, how could he not? He's in charge of the watermelon and a hungry metre-wide male tortoise called Speedy is lumbering towards him.

While we're having a wonderful time at the zoo, Rusty has dragged Mum to Battle Beast Universe after a quick stop at Clarence

Caring's house. Battle Beast Universe is the only place in the country where he can see his favourite Battle Beast miniatures blown up from seven-centimetre models into two-metre monsters. I bet he hasn't shut up about amazing dioramas and sweet paint jobs. Poor Mum.

"We get to muck out the giraffe enclosure next!" I shout to Dad.

"Super," says Dad, rinsing watermelon juice off his hands with the hose used for topping up the lagoon pool.

After he's dried his hands, I chuck him my phone.

"Take a photo of me," I say, posing beside Speedy.

He takes a couple of quick snaps then looks at his watch. "Goodness, we've been here for five hours!"

"Five hours! It feels like five minutes!" There are still so many animals to see. "I'm definitely getting a job here when I'm older."

Dad hands my phone back. "You go with the rest of the group. I'm going to get changed ready for the Guild event. I'll meet you at the giraffe enclosure after you've dealt with the muck, okay?"

I'd forgotten about the Guild. Talk about putting a downer on the perfect day, but it will make Dad happy, and he deserves that. Especially after being zombified by the Cinderman only weeks ago. I don't want to think about what life would have been like if Rusty and I hadn't been able to save both our parents. If putting up with an unexciting evening at the Guild is the price we pay, then that's okay. But for now, I need to get on with giving Speedy a bath.

The rest of the afternoon disappears in a flash and all too soon, I'm being handed my keeper certificate and badge.

"Do you want to smarten up?" asks Dad.

"These are my best dungarees," I say indignantly.

He lets it go and hurries me towards the tube.

"Come on, Indigo," says Dad, as we climb the escalator. "People don't get an invitation to the Guild every day. Trust me when I say that it is something very special."

I appreciate that Dad joined in with all the animal stuff when it's not his thing, so I keep my doubts to myself.

But now that I'm not distracted by London Zoo and all the amazing animals, the invitation is playing on my mind. If it's such a distinguished organization, shouldn't it have fancy invitations that don't smell like an ashtray and look like they're going mouldy?

We exit the tube into the middle of Waterloo Station. It's packed, people of every shape and size rushing everywhere, carrying bags and rucksacks or pulling suitcases. Even the air is crowded with the hum of voices, the thump of feet and the distant rumble and screech of the trains.

The only things keeping their distance are London's ghosts.

Dad's oblivious to all the ghost stuff because he and Mum have no sixth sense whatsoever, but I'm a Spooksmith. We rank ghosts from one to five depending on their strength and ferocity. The ghosts haunting this station must only be Category Ones and Twos. I know this because my goosebumps are mild and I'm not shivering. However, most phantoms love finding someone who can see and hear them because they want help. Yet this lot? They just hover at the edges of my sightline. It's like they're deliberately keeping away from me. Why?

Back home in Greyscar, ghosts seek Rusty and me out. We're even friends with some of them, like Chuckles the phantom toddler. But here in a city of millions, I'm being avoided. It was the same at the zoo, although I was too focused on the animals to really pay attention.

Curious, I smile and try to catch a ghostly eye to see if that changes anything. The only thing it changes is that I lose sight of Dad in the crowd. My hand tightens on my zoo-gift-shop bag. I don't know this place and I don't want to get lost...

Maybe the ghosts here can help. They're starting to creep closer. One of them, a tall male ghost with a pimply face, looks like he's about to ask me something.

"Indigo!" shouts Dad.

The ghost skitters away as Dad's arm reaches out of the crowd and a smoky smell wraps around me.

"Keep up!" says Dad.

He takes my hand and pulls me after him like a little kid. For once, I don't fight him. If I don't have to worry about where I'm going, I have time to think.

It seems like the ghosts weren't keeping away from me, they were keeping away from Dad. But why? He has no powers whatsoever... Then it hits me – the smoky smell. The Guild's invitation. I knew there was something odd about it and now I'm certain that's what has spooked London's ghosts, just from sensing it in Dad's pocket. And if they're reacting so strongly, that must mean that whatever is waiting for us isn't just bad, it's very bad.

Mum and Rusty are meeting us at the Guild HQ – we need to get there as soon as possible so I can warn Rusty and we can work out what to do.

By the time we reach Westminster Bridge Road, I'm the one pulling Dad along.

"I'm glad you're eager to get there," says Dad. "But I don't want to arrive a sweating mess." He pauses beneath the flickering street lights to brush down his suit and I spot Mum and Rusty.

They're standing outside a four-storey building. The top floors are all fancy red bricks, decorated with gargoyles, while most of the ground floor is taken up by a dirt-splattered, grey stone arch big enough to fit a bus through. There's a driveway running beneath it, but I can't see where it goes.

I exhale. Mum and Rusty are okay. For now. I just need to change Mum and Dad's minds about going inside this potential hellhole.

There are no lights on. There's also no obvious way in. Black metal bars with spikes are between us and the building. They don't exactly spell out *Welcome*.

"It looks shut. Maybe we should just call it a day and find somewhere for dinner?" I suggest hopefully.

Mum wipes the dirt from a brass plaque with the end of her brightly coloured scarf.

"This is the address on the invitation: 121 Westminster Bridge Road," she says.

"Battle Beast Universe is only around the corner," says Rusty, perking up. "We could go back. You'd love the Destiny Desolation and Fanged Fracas exhibits. And look at this sweet T-shirt I picked up in the sale bin." He opens his coat to reveal a snot-green T-shirt with the head of some ugly monster printed on it.

"We are not going back there," snaps Mum. Looking

desperate, she steps forward and rattles the bars. There's a *click* and a gate swings open.

"Ha! A hidden entrance!" says Dad, suddenly all positive. "The Guild are known for being very secretive. Couldn't have everyone just turning up on their doorstep."

"As if everyone would want to," says Rusty.

"I really don't think this is a good idea—" I begin.

"Enough of the negativity," Dad says sternly. "This is my big moment. The Guild was formed by three funeral-directing families back in the 1700s. Only a handful of other families have ever been asked to join. To think that their descendants have seen fit to put Serenity Funerals on the same footing as Snarfit & Sons and Mawkish Memories is quite something. If we are accepted, we'll get to display the gold coffin stamp. It's a bit like getting a royal warrant..."

I've stopped listening, but Dad is still chattering to Mum like an excited child. I want it all to be true, but my Spooksmith senses are telling me to be very, very careful.

I look at Rusty.

"Parents," he says, and shakes his head disapprovingly.

"You're picking it up too, right? Something's wrong."

Rusty nods. "Who invites people to a party, turns off all the lights and doesn't even open the door?"

"It's not just that. Ghosts have been avoiding me, and I

think it's because of the invitation. It's like they know who sent it and don't want to go near it."

Rusty shrugs. "It is pretty stinky—"

A door bangs shut on the other side of the gate, making me jump, but it's nothing compared to the shock I get when I notice that Mum and Dad are no longer beside us.

"They've gone in," I say, eyes widening. Wrongness is streaming off this place like the stink from a skunk, but it seems like Rusty and I are the only ones picking up on it.

"And they call us irresponsible," says Rusty.

"Come on, before something haunts them."

3

We step through the gate. To the left is a curved building. To the right, the cobblestoned driveway dives beneath the grey stone arch. The walls beneath the arch are tiled in green bricks and lit by old-fashioned, lantern-style lights.

It's a strange, sickly light, the kind that makes everyone look pale and ill, but that's not the only thing worrying me – there's a hum in the air like static. When I listen harder, the hum turns into distant voices all talking over one another. Like the phone calls we kept getting at home. My skin turns into goosebump central.

I grab Rusty's arm. "Can you hear that?"

"Unfortunately, yes I can," says Rusty. "It seems we've found the most haunted building in London."

I take a little packet of salt out of my pocket and see Rusty do the same. Neither of us ever go anywhere without it. Salt is a solid ghost defence and it's easy to carry, but we have better ones. I'd kill for a giant can of lavender Smell Fresh air freshener right now. It has some serious ghost-blasting capabilities.

Stepping over the rotten threshold of the curved building, we enter a cobwebby entrance hall. The gaslights on the walls reveal wood panelling and a rickety staircase. The only sign that Mum and Dad have been here are two sets of footprints on the stairs.

"I'm not getting posh and important Guild from this place," says Rusty. "And it's blummin' freezing."

We both know what that unnatural drop in temperature means – ghosts. This isn't always a bad thing – most ghosts are friendly when you get to know them – but today I'm picking up bad energy.

There's a bench curved around one wall and opposite that a small window beside an open door.

"Nice," says Rusty, peering through the door. "I'd give it a solid six on the we-should-probably-run scale."

The room through the door is tiny, just enough space for a chair and a desk, both of which have been tipped over. There are piles of paperwork and rolls of unravelled tickets everywhere.

So far so shabby. The really disturbing thing is the writing on the walls:

Death comes to all

I shiver.

"What is this place?" asks Rusty.

"I don't know and I don't like it. I knew that invitation was bad news."

"Why didn't you say anything?" asks Rusty.

"You and Mum and Dad were so excited about this trip... and then Mum mentioned the zoo." It's a weak excuse. I should have tried harder. But I didn't. I change the subject. "Who do you think sent the invitation?"

"Someone looking for fun and friendship," says Rusty, his voice dripping with sarcasm. He points to the footprints in the dust ahead of us. They lead up the stairs.

"Must be them, right?" I ask.

"Or a hideous four-legged monster." Rusty grins, but I can tell he's worried from the way he's twisting his coat sleeve.

I tear open my packet of salt, cursing myself for not packing any other defences. I'm not sure a set of sloth pyjamas and a tiger toy from the zoo gift shop will cut it against an army of the dead.

We follow the footprints up to the first-floor landing where two signs shaped like bony fingers point in opposite directions. One gestures further up the winding stairs towards *Private Offices*, the other straight on to *Waiting Rooms*.

Rusty tugs on my sleeve and whispers, "We're in a hospital."

I don't have any better ideas, but I'm not so sure. That doesn't explain the ticket office. Why have we been invited here and by who?

We follow the footprints in the dust along a door-less corridor leading to another set of stairs. They go down, leading outside to an L-shaped courtyard which ends in a brick wall. Off all the other sides are low buildings with green doors displaying brass *Waiting Room* plaques.

There are still no visible signs of any ghosts, but from the moment we arrive in the courtyard the whispering of the dead gets louder.

"They're getting excited."

"It's definitely giving off that 'dead and looking to party' feel," says Rusty. "What do you say to finding Mum and Dad and then getting out of here?"

"You check the left side; I'll take the right."

"Mum!" shouts Rusty, throwing open the first waiting room door.

"Dad!" I shout, bursting through another one.

The room is empty, except for the wooden benches around the walls, a small black fireplace and a central table. Every door I open reveals a room identical to the first. What is this place?

Mum and Dad must be here somewhere, so I carry on searching. I finally spot something sticking out from behind a pillar on the other side of the courtyard. It looks like the edge of Mum's yellow coat.

"There they are!" I shout, and point.

We both drop our bags and head towards them.

"Mum!" Rusty shouts. "Dad!"

Our parents don't move. It's like they're frozen. There's a smoky smell in the air which I'm sure wasn't there before and there's a new sound I can't place, a sort of huffing and puffing drowning out the whispers of the dead. My skin is prickling, every sense telling me to run.

"Something's coming and I don't think it's something good."

"Grab and go!" Rusty shouts.

But there's no time. With a roar of steam and smoke, a train crashes through the wall and into the courtyard. It's an old-fashioned steam train with a boiler and chimney and the force of its arrival blasts Rusty and me backwards. We hit the wall behind us, bouncing off it and hitting the floor.

Rusty is knocked out. Our packets of salt spill uselessly onto the concrete. My head is throbbing, but my eyes are out on stalks because although it had the power to knock us over and smoke is choking my lungs and stinging my eyes, this train is cold and grey and see-through.

What little breath I have left in my body catches in my throat as I realize what I'm looking at. It shouldn't be possible…the train in front of me is a ghost train.

There's a rumble of ghostly voices and the faint hissing of steam. The sounds drift in and out of reach and I fight to stay conscious. I need to rescue Mum and Dad. I can't lose them again…

My vision blurs as I try to stand. I lie back down to stop myself from passing out. Cheek against the concrete, I watch the train door opposite Mum and Dad creak open.

All I want to do is to scream a warning, but I only manage a whispered, "No."

A veiled apparition in a long black gown leans out of

the door, spiking a memory. I've seen this ghost before, but my brain is refusing to connect the dots and Mum and Dad aren't helping. They just stand there, faces as blank as Rusty's plastic models. They look the way they did when the Cinderman took control. They look like zombies.

It can't be happening again... I push myself up on arms as weak as spaghetti.

The veiled ghost beckons them with a pale and bony hand. The rings on its fingers clink together as the hand moves, like a creepy wind chime.

"Don't!" I wheeze, not that Mum and Dad pay any attention.

They step aboard. And then the really terrifying thing happens. From the moment their feet meet the train, they start to change, their bodies becoming less solid and more transparent, like they're leaving the living world behind. I stagger forwards, battling my woozy head and bruised limbs. I must get to them before...

The door slams shut, the train whistles, steam filling the air. Then the wheels start to turn.

"Stop!" I splutter, reaching for my parents as the train moves back through the wall, following the direction of long-vanished tracks.

The ghostly passengers on the train turn towards me and

raise their hands. My heart rises with them. Are they going to help? Then their hands begin to move from side to side and I realize what they're doing – they're waving goodbye.

"No!" I scream.

It does no good. The train, the ghosts, and Mum and Dad vanish in a puff of smoke.

4

It doesn't matter how many times I hit the wall; I can't break through like the ghost train did. I scream their names; there's no answer. Mum and Dad have disappeared, and all Rusty and I are left with are bruises and soot marks.

At least when the Cinderman turned them into zombies they were still physically with us. Now they've been whisked away by a ghost train; it's like they were never here. We don't have anyone to help us this time either – no Phrank, or Grandpa, or any friendly ghosts. We are totally and utterly alone.

There's a moan behind me. Rusty is sitting up, rubbing his head.

"Tell me they didn't get on that train," says Rusty.

A lump is forming in my throat: one minute Mum and Dad were here and the next, gone. I don't trust myself to speak without crying.

Rusty can tell from the look on my face that the news isn't good. He slumps against the wall and I join him. The adrenaline is draining from my body like water down a plughole. I'm concentrating hard on the ground to stop the tears when I see them – two pale green squares of paper about the size of a matchbox. They're lying on the ground beside Rusty's legs. He spots them at the same time I do, and we each pick one up:

Necropolis Railway
One-Way Coffin Ticket
Third Class
Waterloo to ~~Hollow Hills Cemetery~~ *Necropolis City*

"This place isn't a hospital," says Rusty. "It's a station."

"A station for the dead," I finish with a shiver.

I turn the ticket over.

Scrawled in small, black, spidery handwriting are the words:

> To save your parents, whistle for the train.
> I'm dying to put you to work.

"Someone did this to get to us." Rusty's fingers curl over the ticket, making a fist.

"We've been set up," I agree. "From the moment that invitation arrived, someone else has been pulling the strings."

"Whoever they are, they've done their homework," says Rusty. "They knew Dad couldn't resist an invitation from the Guild. It's almost as though they were watching us."

"Or listening," I add with a shiver.

"The phone calls," we both say at the same time.

Specifically that last phone call on the day the invitation arrived. Dread settles in the pit of my stomach. "There was someone there, in the hall mirror, before I answered the phone. I think it was the same someone who just pulled our parents aboard that train."

"Someone was *in* the mirror?" says Rusty, sitting up straighter.

"It was just an outline. I switched the light on, and it disappeared. I didn't think any more of it at the time—"

"What did this 'outline' look like?"

My mouth is dry. "A veiled woman."

Rusty puts his ticket in his pocket and takes out a strawberry lollipop. He pops it in his mouth. It's not quite as distinguished as Sherlock Holmes with his pipe, but I'm sure it smells better.

"This veiled woman has been trying to get our attention," he mumbles round the side of the lollipop. "This is a kidnap – or rather a parent-nap."

"The only good thing is that Veil Face has to keep them alive, or we've got no reason to accept her very unkind invitation," I add.

"The question is, what does she want?" Rusty asks.

"The Cinderman wanted revenge on all Spooksmiths and to be restored as the one true master of Greyscar. Veil Face wants to put us to work, but doing what?"

"I'm sure it's something lovely like helping her rescue orphans or building an animal hospital," says Rusty sarcastically.

I shrug. "We don't have much choice if we want to save Mum and Dad."

"Then we do as she asks," says Rusty. "We whistle, but not before we've stocked up on supplies."

* * *

Five minutes later and we're in the corner shop on Westminster Bridge Road.

"They've only got three canisters of lavender air freshener and none of them are my preferred brand," Rusty calls over a shelf of cleaning products.

Lavender is a brilliant ghost defence. Put it in a spray can and it's unbeatable. Salt and sage are right up there too. All three ingredients burn ghosts, which is something I usually want to avoid, unless, you know, that ghost is trying to kill me.

"Better than nothing," I say. "I've got the sage, just looking for salt."

I locate a miniature plastic salt and pepper grinder set behind an ancient packet of dried oregano. I'm just returning the oregano when a trickle of cool air hits my back.

Behind me stands an old woman with her hair in a tight bun. She has glasses on a chain around her neck and she's carrying a basket. All completely normal. Apart from the fact that she's also completely see-through.

I swallow, force away my look of surprise and pull my mouth into a smile. It's my "friend to all ghosts" face.

"Hi," I say. "I'm Indigo. Can I ask you a few questions?"

The woman blinks at me.

I try again. "I'm trying to find out about the Necropolis Railway—"

At the mention of that name, the woman shoots through the door, creating a draught that makes the lights rattle.

So much for being friendly. I make my way to the till.

Rusty's waiting for me there. He's holding the lavender air freshener, a bag of crisps and a packet of cookies too.

"Who were you talking to?" he whispers.

"There was a ghost by the oregano," I whisper.

At the mention of the word "ghost", the teenager behind the counter looks up from his *Gravediggers* comic. He's got the thin, wispy beginnings of facial hair and a badge on his T-shirt with the name *Mikey*.

"Did you say 'ghost'?" he asks.

I shake my head and take my card out to pay.

"I get some pretty weird vibes from this place sometimes," continues Mikey. "I'm an expert on the paranormal. Learned it all right here." He stabs his finger down onto a picture of a blood-oozing ghoul in the comic.

"That's nice," I say, picking up our shopping while urging Rusty to do the same.

"You need to be careful out there. Westminster Bridge Road is one of the most haunted streets in London," says Mikey. He's smiling now.

If he's deliberately trying to freak us out, he's picked the wrong people.

"Watch out for cold spots," I say, shoving our shopping into a bag.

"And if you get unexplained goosebumps, run," adds Rusty.

"Yeah, right!" Mikey laughs.

We leave the shop, but as we walk past the window, I see Mikey shiver. The ghost of the old lady is back and she's reading the comic over his shoulder.

The Necropolis Railway building looms ahead. Just the sight of its gloomy, grey archway makes us stop. We're about to board a ghost train to save our parents from a veiled ghost with zero backup other than some toiletries and seasoning. I'm not afraid to admit, I'm scared.

We walk back through the station to the platform.

"We need to whistle to summon the train," I say. "Ready?"

Rusty nods.

I whistle until my lips go numb and Rusty is just blowing spit bubbles.

"It's not working," he gasps. "Where's the train?"

It doesn't make any sense. Why tell us to whistle if it doesn't work? Is Veil Face making fun of us?

I scout for signs of ghostly activity and my eyes land on the large building facing the archway. The only building we haven't explored yet. It's made of grey stone and has three windows along the side, which are two metres off the ground.

Rusty's eyes follow mine.

"Maybe we need to find a proper whistle, like the one used by a railway guard," he says.

"Maybe we'll find it in there."

It doesn't look like a find-a-train-guard's-whistle type of building. It looks like a chapel, although there's no sign on the wooden door, just a carving of a skull and crossbones encircled by a serpent eating its own tail.

"Ouroboros," says Rusty, peering at the symbol. "It—"

"—represents the cycle of destruction and rebirth." Growing up in an undertaker's means Rusty and I know our life and death symbols. "It looks more like a grass snake than a serpent—"

Rusty rolls his eyes. "Yeah, you've mentioned that once or twice before."

I decide not to let my superior animal knowledge get me into a fight. I peer closer. "There's an inscription: *London Necropolis & National Mausoleum Company*."

"Cemetery and burial chamber enthusiasts, step right this way." Rusty leans round me and throws open the door. I'm hit by the smell of damp, mouldy air. I hesitate, but only for a moment. That faint buzz of ghostly activity is nothing we can't handle.

Inside is a small, dark lobby with two doors leading out from it on opposite sides. There's nothing in here other than a table with several candles on it and a box of matches.

We light one each and turn right into a chapel of rest. It has a high vaulted ceiling and double doors at the far end. There's a table in the middle draped in dusty purple velvet and dead flowers. There's a faint – very faint – tang of lavender in the air. I start sorting through the dead flowers on the central table until I find several stalks of it. You can never have too much in our line of business.

"You seem to have cornered the market in angry flower arranging so I'm going to check out that other room."

"Don't do anything without me," I shout after him.

He's been gone thirty seconds max when I hear a whistle.

I groan. Why can't he do what he's told?

I stuff the lavender in my pocket and hurry out to find Rusty. He's standing behind a desk in a room which is only slightly bigger than our downstairs loo. The buzz of ghostly activity is louder in here and Necropolis timetables and lots of other bits of paper are spread out on the desk in front of him. He's got a big grin on his face.

"Found it!" he says gleefully, jangling the chain of a silver whistle which is now hanging around his neck.

"You might have waited for me before—" I start, but then I

stop, because Rusty is staring at me like I've just transformed into a praying mantis. Then I notice the buzzing from earlier has gotten louder and cold air is snaking around my ankles.

I tense, my heart sinking faster than a rhino in a river.

"There's something behind me, isn't there?"

5

I clench the lavender in my pocket as a stream of ghost-chilled air hits my back.

"Holy Moly..." whispers Rusty, face pale, eyes wide.

"W-what is it?" I ask.

Rusty shakes his head as though what he's seeing is so terrible he can't put it into words.

Somehow this lack of information makes everything ten times worse. My imagination is running wild. I can't take the not-knowing. Eyes wide and unblinking, I peek over my shoulder.

A shimmering swarm of ghostly flies in the shape of a man is behind me. He's wearing a knee-length black coat and peaked cap.

I squeal and vault over the desk to stand beside Rusty.

"*You called?*" A rich voice like you'd expect from a butler on a TV show calls out from within the swarm. The flies stop buzzing long enough for a face to form. Big bushy eyebrows first, then small, darting eyes. These are quickly followed by a full moustache with twirly ends, which surrounds his top lip. It seems an odd thing to think about a face made of flies, but it looks kindly enough.

"We need to s-s-summon a ghost train," stutters Rusty.

The ghost sighs, and flies stream from his mouth. One of them lands on my shoulder. It's a bluebottle – the ghost version of one – its shiny blue-green abdomen dulled to a blue-grey colour. I go to brush it off and my hand travels straight through it. The fly seems unbothered and rubs its face with its leg.

"*I am afraid that is impossible. You are not dead.*"

"Our parents aren't dead either," I say. "But the ghost train took them."

"*Live humans are not taken away by ghost trains. There are rules.*"

"Someone isn't following the rules," I say, crossing my

arms and wishing the creepy ghost fly on my shoulder would buzz off.

The man smiles indulgently like he's talking to a very unintelligent child.

"*I am Malachi Innspectre, Necropolis station master and guardian of the gateway to Necropolis City. Everyone follows my rules.*"

I open my mouth to snap back, but Rusty grabs my arm and shakes his head.

"I've got this," he whispers.

He opens his eyes wide, really working the potential orphan look. He uses it on the teachers at school when he's late handing in his homework. It makes me queasy, but they lap it up.

"How do you explain where our parents are, sir?" says Rusty.

Malachi clears his throat. "*It is quite understandable to struggle to process the loss of one's parents—*"

"They aren't dead!" both Rusty and I shout together.

The flies on Malachi's face start to buzz in agitation. "*How did you get here? This station has been closed since the war.*"

"We were invited to a meeting of The Guild of Traditional Undertakers," says Rusty.

Malachi shakes his head. "*The Guild doesn't exist any more.*

The whole thing must be a mistake. A clerical error. A book-keeping anomaly. An administration blunder..."

"It's not a 'blunder'," I explain. "The invitation was made up to lure us here so a ghost could take our parents. Look."

I show him the ticket with the message scrawled on the back:

> To save your parents, whistle for the train.
> I'm dying to put you to work.

The flies forming Malachi's eyebrows bristle and the one on my shoulder flies off to join them in showing their displeasure.

"What did this ghost look like?"

I explain, and Malachi takes a little ghostly notepad and pencil out of his jacket pocket and begins scribbling.

"A veiled ghost, you say. Can you give more details?"

I tell him everything I can remember.

"No spooks should be returning from the other side. I must launch a full-scale investigation."

"And we'll help you."

Malachi abruptly stops writing.

"You won't be going anywhere. Live humans do not fare well on the dead side."

If Malachi is trying to reassure us, he's not doing a very good job.

"But our parents are live humans," I say.

"They'll be okay, won't they?" asks Rusty, his forehead creased with worry.

"This is all most irregular—"

"Look, just tell us how this ghost train works and what the dead side is, and we'll sort it out." I'm eager to get on with saving Mum and Dad. I'd give up every zookeeper experience day in the world for us all to be back together.

Malachi scowls at us from behind his notepad, then he notices the worry etched on our faces and his own expression softens.

"In 1854, London's graveyards were full. The Necropolis Railway was built to tackle this problem by transporting London's dead to a two-thousand-acre graveyard in the countryside called Hollow Hills. I was lucky enough to work there."

Lucky isn't a word I would have used, but each to their own.

"During the Second World War, and after my death, the Necropolis Railway was bombed. It wasn't thought worth rebuilding it: the glory days of the railway were gone and dealing with London's dead was no longer a problem. The tracks were

dismantled, and the buildings and land sold off. But it wasn't the end, it was just the beginning. The real-life train might have stopped running, but the ghost train was now full steam ahead. My calling had begun."

"What do you mean by 'your calling'?" I ask.

"*I collect and transport London's Victorian ghosts. You might not know this, but ghosts remain because—*"

"—of unfinished business," interrupts Rusty. "It's number one in our list of ghost facts."

"*What a curious thing for children to know,*" says Malachi, raising a fly-formed eyebrow. "*Are you also aware that many ghosts never get the chance to complete that business? This means they become stuck indefinitely. I help them to reach Necropolis City, an in-between place not dissimilar to Victorian London, where they can be amongst their own, dead kind.*"

"What if they don't want to go to Necropolis City?" I ask.

"*I can be very persuasive,*" says Malachi. "*And once the ghosts get there and see how pleasant it is, I doubt very much they would want to come back even if they could.*"

Rusty frowns. "Who makes the rules? Who says no one can come back once they've taken the train?"

"*That would be me, but you'll find my rules are honed through years of experience and are very much in keeping with Victorian sensibilities—*"

"Our parents," I interrupt, not interested in any detail that doesn't involve finding them. "Are they in this Necropolis City, this city that no one is supposed to come back from?"

"The ghost train follows the route of the old Necropolis Railway, with the addition of a new final stop. It goes from Necropolis Station, here in London, to Hollow Hills in Surrey, before travelling through the Vapours to reach Necropolis City on the dead side."

Both Rusty and I are silent as we take this in.

"Does this mean our parents are..." I begin, but can't bring myself to finish the sentence.

"We may still have time to save them," says Malachi, noticing the anguish on both our faces. *"I will put my best agents on it. Agents 666 and 667?"*

Two flies separate themselves from the swarm making up Malachi's ghostly body.

"You know what to do. Board the train, scout Necropolis City for a veiled ghost and the parents of these children. Then report back."

There's no way I'm leaving a couple of flies in charge of our parents' rescue, and from the scowl on Rusty's face, I'd say he's thinking the same thing.

A distant huffing and puffing announces the train's imminent arrival.

"Look," I try again. "We're not just ordinary kids. We can see ghosts. We're talking to you. We're special. We're Spook—"

But Malachi and his flies have left the room.

We both hurry after him to find the train is already beside the platform.

"*Whistle, please,*" says Malachi, holding out his hand to take the whistle from around Rusty's neck.

A silent look of understanding passes between me and Rusty. Malachi is not getting that whistle back and that train is not leaving without us.

We run.

"*Stop!*" yells Malachi, reacting a second too late.

I can hear him buzzing furiously behind us. Rusty pulls ahead. He's getting bigger and faster than me and it's annoying. I'm right behind him, arms and legs pumping, but so is Malachi and his swarm of ghostly flies.

We need the train to go before he can stop it.

"Blow the whistle!" I yell to Rusty.

He whistles and the brakes hiss and the train begins to move back through the wall.

Malachi is closing in, ghostly flies are buzzing around my hair, but I can't get my legs to go any faster.

"Jump!" yells Rusty, leaping to land on a step at the back of the train.

He leans out, reaching for my hand. I stretch my fingers out towards him, horrified to see the gap between us growing. The train is picking up speed and we are running out of time. Two of the three carriages have already disappeared through the wall.

"*Get off that train!*" yells Malachi.

I put my head down and launch myself forward, screaming as I jump, certain I'm about to meet a sticky end. As the wall rushes up to meet me, Rusty's hand grabs my arm and pulls me aboard the ghost train.

6

Somehow, we're standing inside a ghost train. Filmy walls surround us. I'm too stunned to speak. Rusty is standing as still as a statue as though one wrong move will send him tumbling into the black abyss whizzing by beneath our feet.

There's a pale ghostly light inside the train and the interior is old-fashioned, with the carriage divided into different cabins. I know we're moving fast because my legs are wobbling with the vibrations, but outside the windows it's as dark as night.

Occasionally, there's a flash of car lights

or street lights, but mainly we seem to be roaring straight through garages or warehouses and sometimes we're in someone's front room. There's a blurry glimpse of a sofa or a TV and then we're gone.

My head is spinning with the strangeness of it all, not to mention all the questions zooming around my brain.

There are two spooks in the first compartment, one in a top hat and carrying a cane, the other in a stiff black dress and bonnet. They don't look up and we move on until we find an unoccupied section. We sit down carefully on seats that don't look solid enough to hold us but seem to all the same.

"It was bad enough with the Cinderman and the ash and the zombies, but now we've travelled through a wall into… into…" I stare at the darkness outside the window. "Where are we?"

Rusty shrugs. "Malachi mentioned something called the Vapours, but if that's blowing your brain then you maybe don't want to see this."

He holds a trembling hand up, palm towards me, and my stomach lurches.

His hands are turning see-through.

I glance down at my own and gasp when I find that they're the same.

"We started disappearing as soon as we jumped on the train," he says.

I swallow.

"Are we—"

"Dying?" finishes Rusty, saying the word I was trying to avoid. "I don't know."

"That must have been why Malachi wanted to stop us," I say, staring at my hands. They're not ghostly levels of transparent yet, but maybe this is just the beginning.

"Whatever is happening to us will be happening to Mum and Dad too," adds Rusty, his forehead wrinkling with concern.

"Mum and Dad started to disappear as soon as they got on that train. I should have guessed the same would happen to us."

"I don't feel any different though," says Rusty.

"Me neither, but maybe it's only a matter of time."

"Let's get Mum and Dad and get back to the real world before we find out," says Rusty, running his ever-so-slightly see-through hands through his ever-so-slightly see-through hair.

A furious buzzing enters the carriage, and two ghostly bluebottle flies dive at our heads.

"Buzz off!" yells Rusty, swatting at them.

"Don't," I say, letting the bigger one land on the seat beside me. "They're part of Malachi. Agents 666 and 667, right?"

The flies respond to their names. The one beside me furiously taps with a front leg. It makes the same movement several times before I catch on.

"It's using Morse code," I say. Grandpa taught us it two summers ago. Rusty delighted in telling me to "Bog off" using it, but it came in handy when we needed to speak to the ghost of Grandpa.

"Of course it is!" says Rusty, with a manic laugh. "We can talk to ghosts so why not start speaking fly."

"T–U–R–N–B–A–C–K," I translate.

"Well, that's not going to happen," says Rusty, sitting back in his seat and crossing his arms. "We're going to find our parents."

The fly next to Rusty whirs its wings with irritation while the big fly next to me starts tapping his leg again.

"S–T–O–P–T–R–A–I–N–B–L–O–W–W–H–I–S–T–L–E," I translate.

"Good to know," says Rusty, putting his hand protectively on the whistle around his neck. "But I'm still not doing it."

Agents 666 and 667 buzz something at each other, like they're communicating, and then they fly out of our compartment.

"Watch and learn, Indigo," says Rusty proudly. "That's

how you show a pair of flies who's boss."

He twists the whistle chain around his fingers and as he does, I spot something written on the mouthpiece.

"Rusty, can I see that?"

He hands me the whistle.

Engraved on it are the letters *V.S., M.I. and L.W.* Three pairs of letters arranged at the three points of a triangle – it's just like the symbol carved into the crypt wall at home.

I trace the symbol with a fingertip, pushing down hard so that the grooves sink into my soft skin, checking it's really there and not some ghostly trick.

We're part of a line of Smiths with Spooksmith powers, but because our ancestors were weirdly paranoid about people discovering our supernatural skills, no one wrote anything down. We've never known what the symbol or the letters mean apart from it being something to do with our history. And my Spooksmith senses tell me it might not be something good.

"You look like you might be about to vom," says Rusty, moving away. "What is it? Travel sickness?"

The M.I. on the whistle is in bold. My brain has just connected another dot.

I hand him back the whistle. His eyes widen as he reads the inscription.

"It's the same symbol as in the crypt!" says Rusty.

"Exactly. Can you think of anyone with the initials M.I.?"

Rusty scrunches up his face and then his jaw drops open. "You're saying my French teacher, Madame Imbert, is part of the Spooksmith network?"

"No! I meant Malachi Innspectre!" I shuffle closer and point at the inscription on the whistle. "Look, the initials are in bold because it's his whistle."

"Ahh, yeah, I knew that."

He so didn't. Usually, I'd rub his hopelessness in, but I need to get him up to speed.

"So, if these letters are initials, then V.S. surely stands for someone with the surname Smith," I say.

"And that Smith is probably a Spooksmith," says Rusty. "Which just leaves L.W—"

There's a commotion out in the hallway and the two flies come buzzing back in followed by a frowning ghost. He's got a badge saying *Ticket collector* clipped to his stained wool jacket.

He glares at me and Rusty from beneath his peaked cap. A bubble of ghostly spit hangs from his top lip.

"*You two look like you're up to no good,*" he shouts. "*Off my train!*"

"We're trying to find our parents," I say. "Have you seen—"

"*Off!*" yells the ticket collector, spitting everywhere the more animated he gets. "*No tickets, no train!*"

The train slows, pulling into a station called Hollow Hills.

"But we have tickets!" blurts Rusty, rummaging in his pocket. "Here!"

Rusty holds up the little green ticket:

NECROPOLIS RAILWAY
ONE-WAY COFFIN TICKET
THIRD CLASS
WATERLOO TO ~~HOLLOW HILLS CEMETERY~~
Necropolis City

The ticket collector snatches it up.

The flies buzz something in his ear and his mouth pinches into a tight scrunch that looks like a cat's bottom.

"*I can't throw them off the train if they have the correct tickets,*" he growls.

The flies buzz something again.

"*It is out of my hands,*" he says as the train pulls out of the station. Then a sly smile slides across his face. "*But I can kick them out of first class.*"

The flies continue their buzzing as though they are displeased with this outcome, but the ticket inspector just swats them away.

"*Go on,*" yells the collector. "*Get to the other end of the train with the rest of the riff-raff!*"

I stand up, deeply annoyed but trying not to show it.

"We'll go, if you answer my question. Have you seen our parents? My dad's about six foot two inches. He's got dark, wavy hair and always wears a suit—"

"*No!*" yells the ticket collector.

"What about our mum?" Rusty says. "She's the same height as Indigo, but better dressed—"

"*No!*" howls the ticket collector.

"Better dressed?" I hiss at Rusty, as we're shooed down the aisle with cries of:

"*Back of the train, you cheeky beggars!*"

We spend the rest of the journey in a less luxurious setting. The ghostly seats in third class are just simple benches. We talk about Malachi and his potential connection to our family of Spooksmiths, but mostly we worry about what's in our immediate future. Are Mum and Dad okay? How will we find them? What will we have to do to get them away from Veil Face and bring them home?

Agents 666 and 667 buzz around moodily, trying to avoid the attention of several ghostly schoolboys who keep trying to catch them. Their teacher is engrossed in his ghostly newspaper, purposefully ignoring us and them.

Eventually, the boys tire of the flies and start whispering about Rusty and me.

"*They look funny,*" says a boy with holes in his shoes.

"*Maybe they're sick or something,*" says another boy in a too-tight jacket.

"*Oi, miss,*" says the biggest boy. "*What's wrong with you and your friend?*"

Before I can say, *We think we're disappearing because we might be slowly dying,* the boys' teacher snaps his paper shut.

"*Watch your manners, Wallace,*" barks the teacher, glaring first at Wallace and then at me and Rusty.

The atmosphere turns frosty so I'm glad when the train bursts into the light – or rather, the grey gloom. Anything is better than that smothering darkness. Whatever plane we were travelling through felt like being buried alive.

Rusty and I run to the windows to join the schoolboys, who already have their dirty faces pushed up against the ghostly glass.

I blink as my eyes adjust. Four-storey buildings loom over the railway line on both sides, giving it a claustrophobic, "no escape" feel. The grey bricks of the buildings are broken up by skinny windows displaying tatty blinds or rags. Occasionally, the odd figure passes these windows, and the boys stick out their tongues or wave, but the train is nothing special here, so no one gives it a second glance.

I count to ten to calm my nerves and Rusty drums a finger against the windowsill.

The train slows in a squeal of ghostly brakes and steam, and we pull up to the platform where a large black sign declares:

WELCOME TO NECROPOLIS CITY

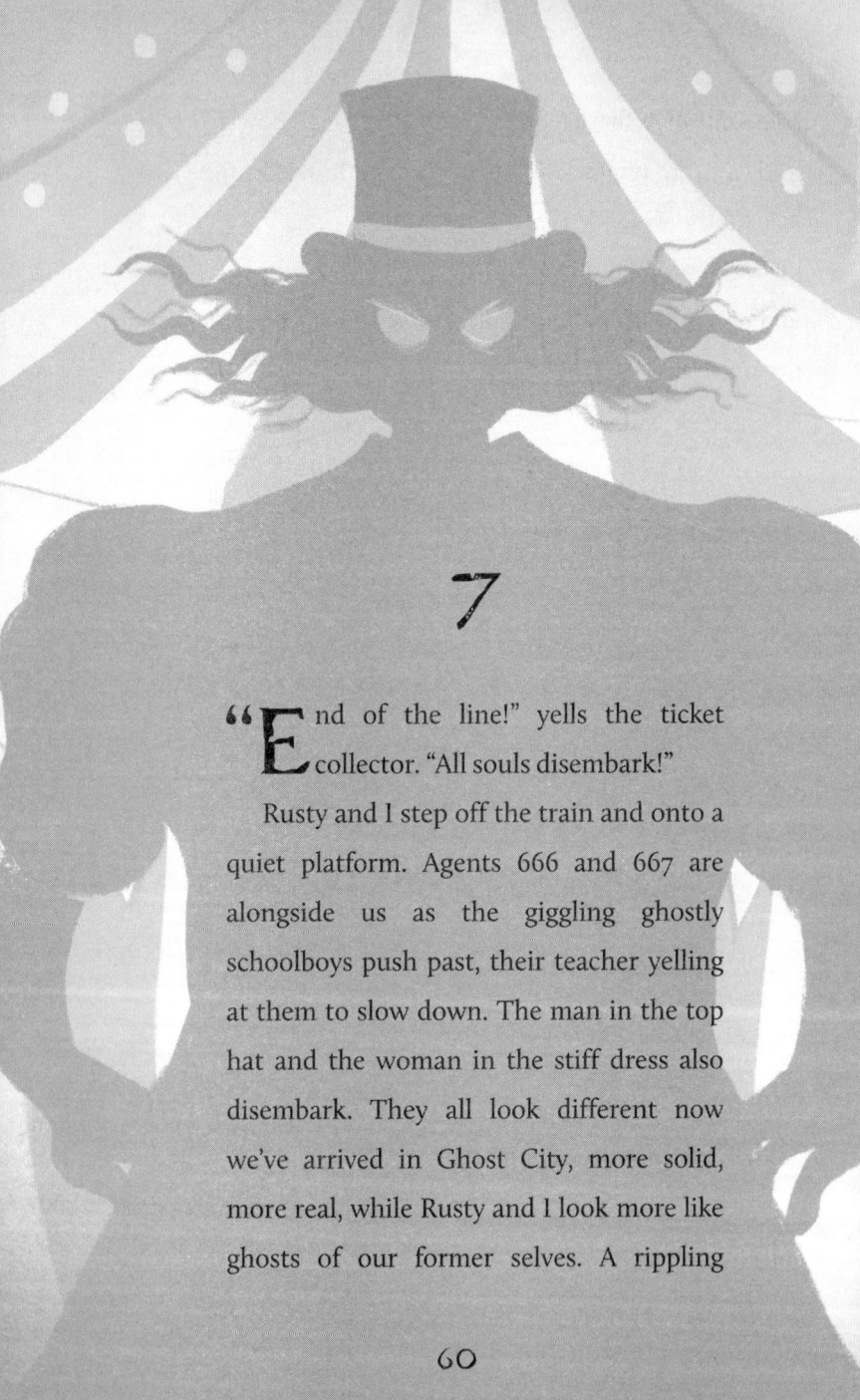

7

"End of the line!" yells the ticket collector. "All souls disembark!"

Rusty and I step off the train and onto a quiet platform. Agents 666 and 667 are alongside us as the giggling ghostly schoolboys push past, their teacher yelling at them to slow down. The man in the top hat and the woman in the stiff dress also disembark. They all look different now we've arrived in Ghost City, more solid, more real, while Rusty and I look more like ghosts of our former selves. A rippling shiver travels from my shoulders all the way down to my feet.

"Rusty, have you noticed—"

"*We're the ones who are disappearing, not the ghosts,*" says Rusty. "*Look at them. They look like normal, living people now we're here. It's like everything has been turned on its head.*"

It's like waking up in a nightmare.

"*I think we're the ghosts now.*"

Rusty pales and stares at his see-through hands. "*Do I sound the same?*"

"*Your voice is fainter...more echoey.*" I can't help but listen to my own faint, echoey voice as I say those words. It's like everything that makes me who I am is being slowly erased. If I think about it too much, my mind will spin out of control.

The woman in the stiff dress stares at us, and the man lifts his cane and points to the writing beneath the welcome sign:

NECROPOLIS CITY RULES:
NO LIVE HUMANS
NO ANIMALS
NO RETURN

"*Victorians might not understand the word 'welcome',*" says Rusty.

"*No place is welcoming without animals,*" I say huffily.

"*What did they have against them?*"

"*Ms Vago said they liked to stuff exotic animals. Or eat them. That famous Victorian scientist Charles Dawkin—*"

"Darwin," I correct him. "*He wrote about how species evolve to survive. I'm not sure how you managed.*"

"*I don't need to evolve.*" Rusty grins. "*I'm perfect just as I am. But that Darwin needed an update. He ate hawks, owls, pumas and armadillos.*"

I remember that now and I wrinkle my nose in disgust. Charles, how could you?

"*Victorians ate loads of filthy stuff,*" says Rusty, clearly on a roll now. "*Bread and dripping, jellied eels and spinach ice cream. Thank goodness I bought cookies and crisps at the corner shop otherwise we might have starved before we disappeared.*"

Rusty rips into the packet of crisps like he doesn't understand the word "wait".

"*We might really need that food later,*" I point out.

"*Well, my stomach says I need it now,*" he argues. "*It's a good sign. If my appetite was disappearing along with everything else about us, then you'd be worried.*"

He has a point. Rusty is always hungry. "*Can you remember anything about the Victorians that isn't food-related?*"

"*Nothing other than places really stank,*" he says through a mouthful of crisps.

"*Helpful,*" I say.

We hurry after the ghosts and into the main station building. It's a big and draughty hall with high-arched ceilings held up by black metal pillars. People dressed in all kinds of old-fashioned and formal clothing – from big puffy dresses to long jackets with tails – are milling around.

Lots of people glance at us then look away, as though we're something nasty that they want to wipe from their minds. It's weird, but not as weird as being stared at. The one boy who is watching our every move is worse. His two front teeth are missing and he's wearing old, holey clothes. He looks a couple of years older than Rusty and me, but it's hard to be sure.

I'm about to tell him it's rude to stare, when the ticket collector sidles up behind us. He makes a sucking noise with his teeth as though he's sizing us up, globs of white spittle forming on his lips.

"Are you sure you're supposed to be here? You look odd and your clothes are all wrong. Necropolis City is for Victorians only. Ghosts must stick to their own timeline."

He moves towards us and I tense. There's no way he's going to put us back on that train before we find Mum and Dad.

I grab Rusty's arm to pull him after me, but Rusty's had

the same thought and he's already moving. We run out of the station into a busy cobbled square, the flies buzzing agitatedly after us.

The ticket collector shouts at us to stop. We don't. We push through street sellers brandishing baskets and newspapers, couples wandering arm in arm, ragged children, and stern businessmen. Our history teachers, Mr Trevathan and Ms Vago, would be lapping this up, but I can't appreciate it because I'm too worried about Mum and Dad – and about me and Rusty too. How long can we last here before we completely disappear?

Ahead of us is a crowd of children, about our age or younger, staring up at a giant clock tower in the centre of the square. It's about half the size of Big Ben's tower with a clock face near the top, but instead of a pointy roof, there's a balcony with a door in it. As we hurry past, the clock strikes six o'clock. I look up to see the balcony door swing open and out creaks a procession of dolls. The first doll is a baby in a pram, followed by a child and then a teenager, all the way through to an old man and woman getting up from their coffins and arriving on a toy train in Necropolis City.

"*Where are we going?*" says Rusty as we push our way through the crowd. We're apparently still solid enough to be an obstacle even though we're a bit see-through.

"*I don't know! I'm just trying to lose that creepy ticket collector.*"

Rusty glances over his shoulder. "*There's no sign of him.*"

We come to a stop on the other side of the crowd.

"*I expected Veil Face to meet us off the train,*" I say.

"*It's weird she didn't when she seemed so keen to drag us here,*" says Rusty. "*Let's ask someone.*"

"*What are we going to say? We don't even know her name! We can't just call her Veil Face,*" I argue.

But before I can stop him, Rusty taps the boy next to him on the shoulder.

"*We're looking for a veiled ghost. Any ideas where we might find her?*"

The boy turns to face us. It's the boy with the missing teeth from the station, although I'm not sure Rusty recognizes him.

"I might know who you're looking for," says the boy with a thin smile.

"*That boy was watching us earlier,*" I whisper.

"*So?*" says Rusty.

Rusty isn't getting my point. There's something about this boy that seems shifty.

"*He could be following us,*" I whisper, but not quietly enough.

"Why would I?" says the boy.

"*Why were you staring at us?*" I snap back.

"You were staring at me!" says the boy.

"*Just give us a minute,*" says Rusty, leading me a few steps away.

"*We've got questions, and I've found someone willing to help,*" says Rusty, a pleading look in his eyes. "*Can you just let it go?*"

I don't have any proof that this boy isn't to be trusted. I give a shrug of acceptance, but silently vow to stay on my guard.

Rusty turns back to the gappy-toothed boy. "*I'm Rusty and this is my sister, Indigo.*"

"Pleased to meet you," says the boy. "I'm Joe."

I'm suddenly aware of how quiet our surroundings are. The clock tower show has come to an end and the square is starting to empty of people.

Somewhere in the distance, there's a low, mournful howl. It makes me flinch.

"*What in the name of Harknock is that?*" asks Rusty.

"*I didn't think Necropolis City welcomed animals,*" I say.

"That isn't an animal," says Joe, something like concern flickering across his face. "We should go."

"*Hang on,*" I say, crossing my arms. "*Go where?*"

But Rusty is already trotting off across the square with Joe. Typical.

The mournful howl is followed by another howl and another. It's a jagged sound that cuts through the evening air, setting my teeth on edge and making my skin crawl. I hurry after Rusty and Joe. They step out of the square and enter a rabbit warren of winding streets.

It's really annoying me that Rusty assumes I'll just follow on like a little puppy dog. I can hear the boys chatting animatedly ahead and despite the howling, I deliberately hang back for a second to see if they notice I'm not with them. Rusty and I are supposed to be a team, a Spooksmith team, and he needs to remember that. We're supposed to make decisions together.

As the houses close in, so does a damp mist and I lose sight of the boys. They still haven't even looked back. I break into a jog to catch them up but when I round the corner, there's no sign of them.

I'm standing alone at an empty crossroads with only the flickering street lamps for company.

"*Rusty?*" I call, spinning around. Where is he?

The answering silence makes the drip of water from the surrounding gutters as loud as a drum. Surely Rusty will notice I'm missing and come back? And where are Agents

666 and 667 when I need them?

The mist thickens like overboiled soup. I can't even tell which way I came from now. My heart starts to thud faster.

"Rusty?"

There's a distant howling, the same as before, but possibly a bit closer. Somehow, knowing it isn't an animal makes it worse, because if it isn't a wild dog or a wolf, what in the netherworld is it?

I raise my fists, showing I'm not afraid of a fight, but whoever – or whatever – is doing the howling obviously isn't afraid either. It's getting closer now and the hairs on the back of my neck are prickling like the spines on a porcupine.

Waiting here to be found no longer seems like an option. Cursing the fact that I've lost my brother now as well as my parents, I pick the right-hand fork at the crossroads, trying to head away from the howling.

I race down another side street full of higgledy-piggledy housing. There doesn't seem to be anyone about – maybe the howler has sent them all into hiding – and soon the buildings become taller, more uniform and industrial-looking.

A few streets on and I'm surrounded by warehouses displaying signs like: EMBASSY ROPE and PICKERING'S PICKLES.

I glance over my shoulder, but the mist is doing a great job of hiding my pursuer. And I'm pretty sure I *am* being pursued. No matter where I've gone, the howling has followed.

I dart left, down an alleyway. It takes me precisely ten footsteps into the mist to realize my mistake.

A two-metre brick wall is blocking my way.

Spinning around, I prepare to run back the way I came, but the howling closes in.

Tears of frustration and fear pool at the corners of my eyes. I rub them away and turn back to the wall, looking left and right, searching for an exit while cursing Joe and Rusty for leaving me behind.

On either side of me are warehouses. There are no doors, and the windows are above my head and barred. This can't end with me trapped like a stray dog. I grit my teeth and try to pull myself up using the bars – if I can just get up there, maybe I can squeeze my way through – but the running has taken all my energy and, after dangling for a few seconds, I let go.

I look over my shoulder.

There are two dark patches at the end of the street, like a hole has been burned into the mist.

Panic squeezes my chest, making me gasp for air. This wall might as well be Everest. There are zero hand- and footholds. I dig my nails into the mortar and try to force my trainers into a non-existent gap. But no matter how much

I kick and scrabble I can't find any grip. My pulse thumps a warning, and I slide back down to the cobblestones.

There's another eerie howl from the mist. There's only one thing for it. I have to face whatever is after me. Determined to take control of this situation, I pull the only weapon I have from my dungarees pocket: lavender air freshener. I release a blast into the mist.

There's a howl of disgust, but no sign that I've inflicted any damage on whatever is after me. Rusty's got the salt and sage. I've got no other defences and nowhere left to run. This was supposed to be a rescue party. Some rescue. What will happen to Mum and Dad without me? What will Rusty do? He'll never survive on his own...

A rope thumps down the wall beside me. I blink. That definitely wasn't there before.

"Up here!" shouts Joe from the top of the wall.

As if I need to be told. I'm already halfway up it and I don't look back.

Joe takes off as soon as I reach the top, sprinting across the bricks as nimbly as a cat. Shaky from the climb, I race after him, jumping to join him on a platform with a winch and a wooden door. It's a good thing I'm not scared of heights because we're as high as two grizzly bears standing on their back legs.

Joe fiddles with the lock and slides the door back.

I step inside the warehouse and Joe shuts the door behind us. It's pitch black until he lights a candle.

"*Where's Rusty?*" I ask. "*And what are those things in the mist?*"

"He's somewhere safe and those 'things' are Death Shadows," Joe answers matter-of-factly. "Their job is to keep the dead and the living apart. By any means necessary. They only appear when someone is breaking the rules – like a ghost not sticking to its own timeline or the living breaking into the land of the dead…"

"*What happens if they catch you?*" I ask.

"Rogue ghosts are obliterated," says Joe with a shudder. "But I'm right where I'm supposed to be, so I'm all right. You on the other hand are a live human; you're all see-through. If they catch you, they'll suck the life out of you."

I shiver.

"What were you doing winding them up with that filthy scent? No wonder you made them mad. It ruddy stinks!"

"*You're not scared of lavender?*"

Joe shakes his head.

"*What about salt or sage?*"

"Did you get a bump on the head back there?"

My temper flares, but he's answered my question. The

71

ghost defences Rusty and I know about are useless here in the city of the dead.

The adrenaline from the chase drains from my body and exhaustion hits me. How are we going to save Mum and Dad from a ghostly horror if we have no weapons?

8

Joe hurries me through the misty streets of Necropolis City and away from the Death Shadows. We pass stalls selling roasted chestnuts and jellied eels. They smell of nothing, which in the case of jellied eels is probably a good thing, but it's strange not to get a whiff of anything. It must be another quirk of this place.

"*So where is Rusty?*" I ask.

"The Death Shadows weren't only after you," he says. "I hid him."

I walk faster. I hadn't thought that Rusty might be in danger too.

"*Is he close?*"

Joe gives a little bow and gestures towards a red-bricked building with an iron canopy over the entrance. The sign says EMPIRE THEATRE, but the windows are dark.

"*In there?*" I ask, peering into the darkness.

"I know all the best places," he says, giving me a wink, like this is just a bit of fun.

He disappears round the side of the building and I follow. The stage door is locked but he leads me through a small delivery hatch, like a large cat flap, at the base of the door.

"Ta-da!" he says, as we get to our feet inside.

I'm not sure what he's so impressed about – it's dark and cold and... Rusty's Battle Beast war cries echo down the deserted corridor.

He sounds scared.

"*Son of Smite!*" Rusty yells, followed by a crash.

I sprint down the dark corridor and past several dressing rooms with chipped red doors towards Rusty's cries.

"*Take that, Spawn of Satanya!*"

Rusty is centre stage, furiously yelling and throwing bits of scenery at a howling patch of moving darkness. I know without Joe telling me – it's a Death Shadow and it's closing in on my brother with a ravenous hunger.

Rusty takes out his can of lavender air freshener. He doesn't know it's worse than useless. I try to run forward to help, but Joe pulls me back behind a red velvet curtain.

"*Get off!*" I snap.

"There's another way to save him that might not get you both killed," whispers Joe. "Death Shadows devour the living, remember?"

He pulls down hard on the lever to his right. With a scream, Rusty drops through a trapdoor in the stage. Joe pushes the lever back up, the trapdoor closes, and the Death Shadow is left empty-handed and howling.

Clever. Not that I have time to tell Joe that. I'm down the stairs and beneath the stage like a shot.

"*Rusty?*" I whisper into the cobwebby darkness.

"*Over here,*" he whispers back.

I crawl beneath the boards to find Rusty sitting up on a pile of old costumes, rubbing his head.

"*I thought that was it,*" he says.

"*It still might be if we don't get out of here quick,*" I say.

"*What is that thing?*" says Rusty.

"I'll explain everything later," says Joe, crawling in to join us. "But right now, I need to get you two somewhere safe." He eyes up the costumes and then tosses us both a set of bonnets and puffy dresses. "Put these on. They might help hide your life force."

"*Life force?*" I splutter.

"It's pouring off you," says Joe. "And it sparkles. The Death Shadows are drawn to light... Look, I said I'll explain later. Just do as I say unless you both want to end up—" He pulls a finger across his throat.

We struggle into the costumes and then crawl after Joe, which is more difficult in a long dress. It keeps getting caught around my legs and all the while I can hear the Death Shadow howling as it searches the stage above us. Beads of sweat gather on my forehead at the thought of dying. Would we become ghosts in another Necropolis City from our own timeline, or would we just blink out of existence? Neither appeals.

We creep out from under the stage, back into the corridor with the dressing rooms. Joe goes through a door marked *Players Privy* into a bathroom. The floor is tiled in black and white and the walls in green and white. There is one cubicle, two urinals and one sink. There are no windows or other doors.

"*What now?*" asks Rusty, adjusting his bonnet.

I put my hands on my hips. "*Well, it seems that Joe here has led us into a dead end.*"

"Not true," says Joe, grinning. He lifts a grate in the floor revealing a dark hole. "Your way out, m'lady."

It's a drain. In a bathroom.

"*You've got to be kidding,*" I say. "*I'm not dropping into a sewer.*"

"Suit yourself," says Joe, crossing his arms over his chest and dropping into the hole.

"*There's no way,*" I say, wrinkling my nose even though there's no smell.

A howl sounds right outside the privy door.

"*Bottoms up!*" whispers Rusty, and he launches himself after Joe.

Oh, for goodness' sake, I'm not losing him again. I lower myself into the hole. As soon as I let go of the tiled lip, I start to slide downwards. Slowly at first but then picking up speed until I'm zooming like a penguin on ice. I try hard not to scream as I shoot out of the tunnel and land in a puddle of water. At least, I hope it's water.

Joe strikes a match and takes a candle from his pocket. The flame flickers, illuminating a vast underground brick tunnel with a shallow stream of water running along the bottom. If I stand on tiptoes, my fingertips still can't reach the roof and it's at least two arm spans wide.

"There once was a man named Rob Ride," says Joe. "Who fell in the sewer and died.

"The same day his brother, fell into another, but he just swam to the side."

Both boys are giggling away together, and Rusty is adding new lines to the limerick. I get a pang of jealousy.

"*That was disgusting,*" I say, brushing myself down.

"*There are no number twos here,*" says Rusty, still grinning.

"*Like you know everything,*" I snap. My bottom is wet from the slide, I'm annoyed at Rusty for getting separated from me, I'm worried about Mum and Dad and I'm one hundred per cent terrified of those life-devouring spirits. Add it all together and it doesn't equal a good-mood day.

"He's right," Joe defends him. "Necropolis mostly mirrors Victorian London, sewers and all, but you know, ghosts don't need to—"

"*Okay, I get it.*" I don't need Joe to tell me ghosts don't use the bathroom.

I look back up the tunnel we just slid down. "*Can those things find us down here?*"

"It's best we keep moving," says Joe.

"*Where are you taking us?*" I ask.

"Back to the station," he says. "It's not safe for you here."

Rusty and I stop walking.

"*We're not going home.*" I can't even compute the idea of going back without Mum and Dad.

"*We came here to rescue our parents,*" says Rusty. "*That's why I asked you about the veiled ghost who kidnapped them.*

You said before that you might know who it is..."

There's a long pause.

"I know who took your parents," says Joe quietly.

There's no hint of his usual "cheeky chappy" persona and no jokes. I find it rather worrying that the ghost to subdue him is the one who's taken Mum and Dad.

"*If you know who it is, please tell us,*" begs Rusty.

Joe turns away, so his face is hidden in shadow. "The ghost you're looking for is Hell Mary."

9

The name Hell Mary sends shivers down my spine.

"*Is it one of those joke names?*" asks Rusty. "*Like when you call someone little and they're actually really big?*"

Joe shakes his head. "Hell Mary is no joke. She was a fortune-teller when she was alive. In the living world it's rumoured that if you say her name three times into a mirror, she'll appear in the glass."

"*What is it with ghosts and having their names spoken aloud?*" I ask. The Cinderman was the same, although you didn't have to say his name three times for him to grow stronger. Once was enough.

"*And if you repeat her name the right number of times,*" Rusty prompts, "*what happens then?*"

"She'll show you your future," explains Joe. "Or she'll scratch your eyes out."

Rusty and I stare at each other in stunned silence.

"*Personally – and this could just be because I don't have a thing for eye gouging – I don't think summoning her is worth it,*" says Rusty.

"*Hard agree,*" I say.

"Are you sure you want me to take you to her?" asks Joe.

"*Hell yes,*" says Rusty, without a moment's hesitation.

"*However bad Hell Mary is, we don't have a choice,*" I say. "*She wants something from us, and we want something from her – Mum and Dad.*"

I swear I see Joe's shoulders sag like he's disappointed by our decision.

"It's this way," says Joe, and he turns down a smaller, brick-lined tunnel to our right. "If you're sure…"

As we walk on, we grill him for information about Hell Mary.

"*What do you think she wants from us?*" asks Rusty.

"*Does she have any known weaknesses?*" I ask. "*And how powerful is she?*"

Joe answers every question with either, "Haven't the foggiest" or "No idea". His shoulders hunch lower and lower each time he answers.

Eventually, Rusty and I give up on the questions. We drop back from Joe, and I fill Rusty in about the Death Shadows and our defences not working.

"*I feel really sorry for Victorian women having to wear these stupid clothes,*" I say, stepping on the hem of my dress for the hundredth time.

"*How are you supposed to get anything done wearing something that looks like a flouncy lampshade?*" asks Rusty. His dress is smaller and flapping around his knees. But something beyond dresses is bothering me.

"*How did the Death Shadows find us?*"

"I told you before, they track your life force," Joe calls back to us. He's obviously been listening to our conversation. "It's literally streaming off you."

"*I can't see anything,*" says Rusty, checking behind him.

"That's because you aren't dead," says Joe.

We stop complaining about the clothes.

Ahead, a rusted metal grille fills the mouth of the tunnel. On the other side of it is a two-metre drop to a muddy bank.

This leads down to a wide stretch of water. Lights from the surrounding buildings twinkle and ripple like shoals of fish as they reflect off its surface.

"The Other Thames," explains Joe. "We can get out over here."

He pushes hard on the grille and a hinged flap creaks open.

We all crawl through and drop down onto the muddy bank. By the time we reach the pavement above, our feet and the bottom of our clothes are coated in a thick layer of brown silt.

"*If she's a fortune-teller, can't her crystal ball predict this will end badly for her?*" asks Rusty. "*You don't mess with the Sp—*"

"Look, I know no details, nothing about her weaknesses or powers!" snaps Joe, spinning around.

He's weirdly wound up for someone who, until now, has been pretty laid-back. Rusty and I exchange a glance that says, *What's got into him?*

"I can tell you where to find her, that's it," continues Joe, his voice shaking with emotion.

"*You don't need to be scared,*" says Rusty, putting his hand on Joe's shoulder. "*You're with the Spooksmiths now.*"

Joe gives a bitter snort.

"*You* should be scared," he says.

He points to a poster stuck to a lamp post. The edges are ragged, and they flutter in the breeze like the wings of a trapped bird.

I step closer to read the writing:

The Circus of Shadows
Roll up! Roll up!
Clowns, acrobats, mind-readers and past delvers.
Prepare to be amazed!

The picture beneath the writing shows a striped big top tent. Acrobats somersault in front of it and clowns with bright red smiles and deathly white faces grin back at me. And right in the centre – presiding over it all like a spider lying in wait – is the veiled ghost I saw lure Mum and Dad onto the ghost train.

"That's Hell Mary," says Joe.

The knot in my stomach tightens as I stare at the circus poster. Hell Mary is drawn seated at a small round table with a crystal ball in the centre. Every inch of her is covered in black lacy material, except for her bone-white hands.

"Her circus is across the river," says Joe. "Over there."

He points across the fast-flowing water, dark as an oil

slick. I can just make out the curved roof of a big top tent complete with a ragged flag. Even from this side of the river, it's threatening.

I tuck my frizzy curls behind my ears. "*How do you know she'll be there?*"

Joe shrugs and looks at the floor. "She never leaves," he mumbles.

"*Other than to kidnap peoples' parents,*" I say.

"*Oh, come on, Indigo,*" says Rusty. "*She's also busy giving people visions in mirrors and removing eyes. It's a full schedule when you're a professional evil ghost.*"

I smile and thump him on the arm. Rusty can make me laugh even when things are at their bleakest. It's his special skill.

"*I say we sneak in and find Mum and Dad without ever meeting Hell Mary.*"

"*Agreed,*" says Rusty. "*Joe, will you act as lookout? We don't want any Death Shadows sneaking up on us while we're focused on our parents.*"

He nods, unsmiling. The Joe we met earlier was cheerily annoying, but I preferred that version to this one. The fact that he's a ghost and he's scared of Hell Mary is making me anxious.

Like any normal city, there are street lights here, but the

glow from them is an unnatural watery yellow. The lights from the houses and houseboats we pass is the same. It makes everyone, from the street sellers to the smartly dressed couples spilling out of a theatre, look like they've stepped from an old photograph. And then, of course, there's the mist. It rolls in off the Other Thames like the swell of the ocean, meaning that a street can be visible one minute and totally unseeable the next.

The city clock strikes the hour, its chimes reverberating deep in my chest like a warning.

"*Nine o'clock,*" says Rusty. "*We've been here three hours already.*"

"*Three hours too long,*" I say, looking at my faintly see-through hand. Is there a time limit before we become ghosts ourselves? And if there is, what about Mum and Dad? They've been here even longer than we have...

I stare at Joe's back, suddenly irritated. The way he's ambling along makes me think he doesn't want us to arrive.

"*Can you walk any faster?*" I ask.

"If you can keep up," says Joe, picking up the pace. "But I'm keeping a lookout. We don't want the Death Shadows to find you again. It's easier for them to track your life force at night."

"*Why?*" asks Rusty.

"It sparkles in the dark," explains Joe.

"*Great,*" says Rusty. "*I've always wanted to be lit up like an all-you-can-eat buffet.*"

"What's a buff-ay?"

"*Lots of food piled up on a table,*" I say.

"*You can eat anything you want, all on one plate,*" says Rusty enthusiastically. "*Egg and beans, a curry and a chocolate muffin on the side.*"

"Who puts a curry with a chocolate muffin and egg and beans?"

"*I do,*" says Rusty. His stomach growls hungrily and mine joins in despite Rusty's experimental combinations.

Rusty pulls out the packet of cookies.

"*Want one?*" says Rusty.

Joe shakes his head. "Ghosts don't need to eat."

Rusty and I devour the packet. I haven't had anything to eat since lunch.

"*Have you got any other food here before our stomachs attack?*" says Rusty as his stomach gives another loud grumble.

"We do but it's only for show," says Joe.

I have no idea what he's on about. How can you only have food for show?

"*Looks like soup,*" says Rusty, veering across the pavement towards a street vendor. He peers at the watery substance bubbling away in a large metal pot. It smells of nothing, but it certainly looks edible.

Joe stops walking and turns back around to face us.

"Give it a try," he says. He crosses his arms and raises his eyebrows in an *I dare you* way.

Joe gestures to the woman behind the stall. She adjusts her shawl and slops two ladles of soup into two metal cups.

It's comforting to hold something warm, but when I sip it there's zero taste.

"*I'm getting nothing,*" says Rusty.

"*It's like eating a cloud or biting air,*" I agree.

We hand our cups back to the street seller. She scowls and pours the contents of the mugs back into her pot with no regard for food hygiene.

Joe sees me wrinkling my nose.

"That soup has been on the boil since I first arrived here back in 1862," he explains as we walk on. "Ghost food isn't proper food."

"*So why pretend?*" I ask.

"Because we remember what food used to taste like," he says longingly. "I'm never hungry now, but I'm not full either. What I wouldn't give for a delicious slice of mutton pie, or a pot of pickled whelks."

"Roast chicken with loads of gravy," says Rusty, without missing a beat.

"Hot baked potato," says Joe.

"Triple cheese pizza," says Rusty.

"What's that?" asks Joe.

Rusty describes his favourite pizza and by the time he's finished I'm drooling.

"This isn't helping," I say, putting my hand to my stomach. *"Can you talk about something else?"*

Joe cheers up as he tells Rusty about his collection of toy soldiers and Rusty reciprocates with a full-on lesson in Battle Beast. I roll my eyes and leave them to it.

Grand buildings line the river here. They have black railings and steps leading up to smart front doors. It could be a pleasant place to live, but smoke pours from the chimneys all around. It hangs in the air, mixing with the mist to create a thick smog. I'm guessing the dead don't need a fire to stay warm: it's now just a habit, something they've carried over from when they were alive.

We pass lots of people, but no one makes eye contact. They all seem keen to stay away from us, which is fine by me.

A large granite bridge looms ahead, spanning the Other Thames. Ghostly lanterns blink in and out in the distance as they are swallowed up and then spat out by the mist.

We cross the bridge quickly, the water rushing beneath us and laughter carrying on the breeze.

"*How much further?*" I ask Joe.

"Not far now," he says quietly.

The boys don't talk again after that. It's as though my question has reminded them both why we're really here.

Gone are the theatres and the big houses; it's all wharfs and warehouses and the odd pub. It's darker too and the mist seems thicker and heavier, the atmosphere more menacing.

Joe slows down as we approach an open area of marshy ground with only a few ramshackle buildings at the far end.

"Over there," he says, pointing ahead.

The mist shifts and the big top tent is suddenly visible again. Several smaller tents surround it like satellites circling a dying star. The big top canvas has holes in the roof and the red and white striped sides are faded and splattered with mud.

"*Why can't it be an uncreepy circus?*" asks Rusty.

I know what he means. If someone said to design a lair for killer clowns, I'd draw something like this. The flag on top of the main pole hangs at an unnatural angle like a snapped neck and the flapping entrance reminds me of a mouth hungry for its next meal.

I remind myself what we're here to fight for.

"*I want more lectures from Mum on sibling bonding,*" I say, jutting out my chin.

"*I want to be made to clean the inside of the hearse again,*" says Rusty. "*Last time I found half a scotch egg wedged under the coffin runners. Dad ate it.*"

"*That's disgusting!*" I splutter.

Rusty grins. "*Sooo Dad though.*"

It is very Dad. Just thinking about our parents and their funny quirks has given me a warm glow inside. No matter how scary-looking that circus is, we're going in. The key is that we have no intention of being spotted. As Rusty puts it, we're in "stealth mode". If all goes to plan, we'll find our parents and sneak out of there without ever having to face Hell Mary.

We both stride forwards, our feet squelching in the mud, but Joe hangs back.

"*It'll be all right,*" says Rusty with false cheeriness.

Joe doesn't look so sure. "I'll stay here as lookout," he says.

He remains behind as Rusty and I approach the tent.

Soon we're standing at the entrance. Muted applause and a few jeers ring out from inside. Then we slip under the canvas, several metres away from the entrance.

"*What's the worst that can happen?*" whispers Rusty.

"*We might not find Mum and Dad, our eyes could be gouged*

out, and not forgetting the big one: we could die."

"*Is that all?*" asks Rusty.

We ditch the dresses and the bonnets because they're too itchy and they're slowing us down.

Raised wooden seating surrounds a central ring lit by flaming torches. Rusty and I crawl beneath the seats. There are only about ten people in the audience, even though the tent could easily hold about five hundred. There are three female jugglers on the far side of the ring. Their feathery costumes look limp, and they have holes in their tights. A bored-looking man with a humped back occasionally throws them an extra ball to juggle. When one of them catches it, the other jugglers give half-hearted whoops in an attempt to enliven the performance. They flank a man in a tight leotard who is trying, unsuccessfully, to fold himself into a box.

It is the most miserable spectacle I've ever seen, and the audience – what little there is of it – seems to agree. Someone balls up his newspaper and chucks it at a juggler. She yelps and drops one of her balls.

Suddenly a chill descends on the tent.

"CLEAR THE RING!" shouts a rasping voice. It's the sort of voice that sucks all the joy and lightness from a room. It's a voice that is used to being obeyed.

Hell Mary strides into the ring, a giant nightmare in

black lace. And running along beside her, his face pale and twisted with fear, is Joe.

I stare at the scene in front of me, blinking rapidly as I struggle to take in what it means. Joe doesn't seem to be her captive, so what's he doing here? I think back to how he's been behaving since we insisted he brought us here, snapping one minute and then giving us the silent treatment the next. As if he was feeling guilty...

My muscles stiffen, and I clench my fists.

Joe has betrayed us, and it looks like he's been planning on it all along.

10

"I said, GET OUT!" Hell Mary yells.

The performers scatter like mice; the audience too.

"She's got Joe," whispers Rusty, still not getting it. "*We have to help him.*"

I shake my head. I know I had my doubts about Joe, but this...

"*Joe isn't who you think he is,*" I whisper. "*He's a traitor.*"

Rusty's eyes flit between Joe and Hell Mary. I know he's hoping it isn't true. He's too trusting, too gullible even when the ugly truth is staring him in the face.

"*We're friends,*" says Rusty. "*He wouldn't...*"

"*Joe wasn't helping us. He was helping her! He was at the station when we arrived. He followed us. He knew we'd have to ask for help at some point and he made sure he was the one we asked.*"

"Joe tells me that my guests have finally arrived." Hell Mary's voice echoes around the now deserted tent. "Come out, come out, wherever you are!"

She fixes her full glare on the bank of seats we are hiding beneath.

There's only a shadow of a face behind the veil, but even so I recoil. A numbing malevolence streams off her like meltwater from ice.

Rusty and I crawl out from beneath the seats and approach the ring.

"*Joe?*" says Rusty. "*Tell me you're not working with her.*"

My disbelief has turned to outrage. "*He's been lying to us ever since we met him. Pretending to be our friend so we'd trust him.*"

Joe flinches. "I tried to get you to go home."

"*We'd never abandon our parents,*" I snap.

Hell Mary gives a sharp, bitter bark of laughter. She's even scarier up close, even though most of her is buried beneath swathes of black gauzy material. Dangling beneath the veil are several necklaces made of black jet and tiny bird bones. I gulp. The only other visible parts of her are her hands. Each finger is stacked with rings. I flinch as I take in what's decorating them. It isn't jewels or expensive stones, it's teeth. Human teeth.

Rusty looks at Joe. "*Why would you betray us?*"

Joe looks at the floor.

"I told him I could reunite him with his stupid, dead pet." Hell Mary's voice is dripping with distaste.

"Troy's not stupid!" says Joe, finally showing a bit of spirit.

"Maybe not, but you are," Hell Mary scoffs, looming over Joe. "I couldn't summon that rat here even if I wanted to – filthy animals have no souls."

"*Rubbish,*" I say, but no one is listening.

"You promised…" pleads Joe, tears pooling.

He looks broken. I'm almost sorry for him.

"Beasts were always the weakest acts in my circus. I'm glad to be rid of them, although I do miss using Scourge…" She reaches beneath the folds of lace and unwraps a coiled something from around her waist. She flicks it to the side and a black leather whip unfurls with a cruel crack.

"Your services are no longer required." She points the whip at Joe. "Be gone!"

"You promised…" Joe repeats, but he starts to back away,

as though he knows he's already lost.

"Be gone!" She lunges forward and lashes at Joe, striking his shoulder and making him cry out.

Rusty and I are too shocked to react.

Joe turns on his heel and, stumbling and tripping, he runs from the tent. Hell Mary cackles with glee as she watches him go. It lights a fire in my belly.

"*Where are our parents?*" I try to shout, but my voice comes out all thin and reedy and weak.

The teeth on her rings clack together as she folds her whip away.

"I summoned you here because my circus is a shadow of its former self, and I wish to return it to its full glory. To do that, I need something fetching from the living world – my Show Stone."

"*Your what?*" asks Rusty.

"Orbuculum. Gazing Sphere. Crystal Ball... They go by many names. Most of them are mere toys, but mine can show visions of the past and the future."

"*Why can't you get it yourself?*" I ask. I'm pretty sure we're dealing with a Category Five ghost here. The worst of the worst usually are. In the real world they can control the weather, go anywhere they please and zombify people. I'm not sure our categories mean anything here, where all ghosts are solid, but Hell Mary is definitely registering off the scale on evilness.

"I cannot go further than the Necropolis train. My tether is no longer in the human world." She scowls at being forced to reveal this uncomfortable truth about the limit of her powers and reaches for a particularly ugly necklace at her throat. It's made of jet beads and black silk and suspended from it is a mirrored pendant.

"*You don't care about putting us or our parents in danger, do you?*" asks Rusty, interrupting my thoughts.

Hell Mary drums her fingers on her hips, setting the teeth rings chattering. The sound makes my skin crawl.

"You are not in any immediate danger. Although you are weakened by being in Necropolis City, your Spooksmith powers give you some protection. Your parents? Not so much. Ordinary live humans are unconscious and drifting towards death the moment they arrive." She grins nastily.

I bite down on my lower lip to stop myself from crying or screaming. I don't know which; I'm a jumble of emotions. The thought of losing my parents tears me in half, but I'm also burning with rage at Hell Mary.

"I've been watching. And waiting. And listening," says Hell Mary. Her voice is light and amused, as though she's been saving this bit of information and is now savouring our reactions as she shares it. "The line from the other side is truly dreadful, but messages do get through. My overture reached you, did it not?"

So, I was right.

"*You kept calling our house. You sent the invitation. You appeared in the mirror...*"

"I was only a weak reflection of my normal, glorious self because you did not say my name, but yes, that was me."

I can't stand her gloating tone.

"You might have defeated the Cinderman, but you will find I'm not such an easy opponent. Use your powers and work for me by fetching my Show Stone before sunrise, or your parents will pay the ultimate price."

"*Where are they?*" Rusty demands.

I scan the tent, wondering if we can make a run for it and find them before Hell Mary stops us.

"You won't find them." It's like she can read our minds. "I'm very good at hiding things, and I think they'll enjoy some time in my new mirror maze. You have until the tower clock strikes six a.m. to bring me my Show Stone or your parents will die."

"*No!*" shouts Rusty.

Hell Mary smiles. "Shout all you want. It changes nothing."

It's hard to ask this next question, but I need to know.

"*How do we know they're still alive?*" I ask.

"You will have to take my word for it."

"*Like Joe did?*" says Rusty. I'm happy to see some real venom behind his words.

"*You're a monster!*" I hiss.

"You should never be rude to your elders," Hell Mary snaps. "For now, your parents are safe, but I have space for more rings on my fingers. I wouldn't want anything to happen to your parents' teeth..."

Anger takes over and I go to rush her, but Rusty holds me back.

"*You heard her,*" he whispers. "*She'll hurt Mum and Dad.*"

I stop struggling and let myself go limp. "*We'll do what you ask.*"

"Good," gloats Hell Mary, getting to her feet. "You'd do well to listen to your brother. Put that fiery spirit to good use." She removes a ring from her wedding finger. It has an empty space where a stone – or a tooth, knowing her – might sit. She holds it out to me. "The missing tooth on this ring belonged to my soulmate, Seba Smiles."

She pronounces it like "Seb" with a baby "a" sound on the end like the phonics we learned in pre-school. It's a name that makes me think he's not very smiley.

"Seba's remains lie in Hollow Hills Cemetery," continues Hell Mary. "The ring will guide you to him. Tell him I forgive him. Ask him to return to me and as a symbol of his love, to bring me the Show Stone."

I snatch the ring and quickly stuff it in my pocket, not wanting to touch it a moment longer than necessary.

"Return to the station and use the whistle to summon the ghost train," she orders us.

"Remember, the clock is ticking down to sunrise."

With a click of her fingers, Hell Mary disappears, and all the torches go out. We are left in the gloom with just the flapping of the canvas to keep us company and a crystal-ball-shaped obstacle in the way of saving our parents.

11

Outside the big top, the mist has cleared, but my brain is foggier than ever. I don't know how we're going to find our way back to the station, never mind find Seba and the Show Stone using some stupid, empty ring. Not that Hell Mary seems bothered about the details.

The performers we saw earlier have gathered out here. They watch us pass in silence. Ahead, on the muddy path, two ghoulish children are bent over backwards and running around on all fours like broken spiders.

I shiver. They are the stuff that nightmares are made of.

The two children scamper closer until they reach us, blinking up at us through haunted eyes. I fight with myself not to step away.

The children – a girl and a boy – flip themselves out of their backbends. They look similar ages to Rusty and me, just smaller and way more bendy.

"I am Amit," says the boy, wiping muddy hands down his muddy shorts.

"And I am Amira," says the girl, completely unbothered by the dirt. "Are you coming to join our circus?"

I shake my head. *"Hell Mary wants us to fetch her Show Stone."*

At the mention of the Show Stone, all the performers take a sharp breath.

"Do you get the feeling that the Show Stone might be something bad?" I whisper to Rusty.

"We'll never know if we don't ask." He raises his voice to address the perf+ormers. *"If you know anything about it, we'd really appreciate—"*

"It's cursed," says Amit.

"Shh," warns one of the jugglers, her face pale and drawn.

"But it is!" argues Amira, sticking up for her brother.

The humpbacked man who'd been throwing the extra

balls for the jugglers peers out from a small tent. His lantern throws a beam of light across the mud. He's wearing a shirt with the name *Ray* sewn onto the breast pocket.

"If you want my advice, you won't touch that thing," says Ray.

"*Hell Mary has our parents,*" I say.

"*Do you know where they are?*" asks Rusty. "*Hell Mary mentioned a mirror maze...*"

Ray shakes his head. "This place has more shadowy corners than a haunted house. She changes the layout to keep us on our toes."

Rusty's shoulders slump.

"*Why do you all stay and work for Hell Mary if you don't like her?*" I ask.

"Where would we go?" asks Amit, coming closer.

"This circus is all we've ever known," says Amira. "It was beautiful once. People travelled from miles around to visit the famous Starlight Circus in the Hippodrome."

"And then there's the teeth," says Ray.

Rusty frowns, but I think I understand, although I really hope I'm wrong.

"*Hell Mary's rings—*"

"Hold our teeth, one from each of us." He gestures to the assembled performers. "Seven in total." Ray uses a finger to pull up his lip, showing me a gap in his molars.

"*That's level ten disgusting,*" says Rusty.

But it's worse than disgusting. "*Your teeth were your tethers, the things that kept you anchored to the real world,*" I say. "*She took them, and you can't move on without them.*"

"The girl speaks the truth," says Ray. "We're like flies caught in her web. All of us trapped into doing her bidding."

A howl cuts through the night air. I shiver and Rusty jumps. It's a Death Shadow.

"*We need to get back to the train,*" I say.

Amira looks at Ray. "Shall we take them to the ferryman?"

There's a pause as something unspoken passes between them.

"They're children," adds Amit. "Like us."

"Take them," he says, before turning to Rusty and me. "And watch out. Where there's one Death Shadow, more will follow. They rarely hunt alone. But please, if there's another way to save your parents, find it. Don't go near that Show Stone."

"It's bad news," says one of the jugglers.

"Terrible business," says another.

The warning echoes in our ears as we follow Amit and Amira. They move fast, their light, bendy bodies gliding over the mud while Rusty and I stomp on through it.

A second howl picks up when the first one fades, followed by another and another, like a Death Shadow quartet. Fear puts more speed in my legs.

We run on until we reach the Other Thames at the edge of the fairground and slither down the bank onto the muddy foreshore. It's littered with broken planks of wood and piles of rubbish. There's no sign of a ferryman or a boat.

Amira puts her fingers in her mouth and releases a piercing whistle. One of the piles of rubbish rolls over and a man emerges wrapped in a dark cloak. He looks like he should smell, but like everything here, there's not even a hint of a pong.

"You called?" he says, his voice deep and rumbling.

"Basil, were you asleep on the job again?" asks Amit.

"Just a light slumber," replies Basil. "What can I do for you?"

"We need you to get our friends across this river before the Death Shadows get them," says Amira.

I blink. Amira used the word "friends". I'm grateful and a little guilty. The circus performers are trapped under awful circumstances and yet they are helping us even though they don't want us to find the Show Stone. I decide then and there that if I can help them back, then I will.

"It would be my pleasure," says Basil. He starts pushing at

one of the planks of wood and a small, rickety boat slides out and into the water. It looks like a sad excuse for a vessel, but the name written on the side is *The Jolly*.

"Climb aboard," says Basil. "For a fee."

"*Please,*" I say. "*We're being hunted.*"

Basil looks unmoved.

"I just told you they're friends," argues Amira.

Rusty searches his pockets and holds out several coins.

Basil looks disgusted. "I don't want money," he says.

"He collects rubbish," says Amit.

"One man's rubbish is another man's treasure," explains Basil. "I am a collector of ancient artefacts."

"*What about if we promise to bring you something when we return?*" I say, my skin cold and prickling as I sense the approaching Shadows.

"Something interesting?" asks Basil.

"*We'll make sure it's interesting,*" I snap. "*Just get us off this shore before we're dust!*"

"The deal is struck," says Basil.

We clamber aboard and Amit and Amira help us push off as the howling builds to a crescendo. When I look back at the bank, the two children are surrounded by Shadows.

"*Will they be okay?*" asks Rusty.

"The Shadows will not harm the dead who belong here,"

says Basil as he rows us out into the middle of the river. The current is strong, it's tugging the boat downstream, but Basil is stronger. He steers his craft as easily as Dad steers the hearse and within minutes we've reached the other side.

"*Thank you,*" Rusty and I say in unison.

Basil dips his head in acknowledgement. "Do not forget our bargain."

"*We won't,*" I say.

"*Come on,*" urges Rusty. "*Quick, before the Shadows work out where we are.*"

We scramble up the bank to the pavement above.

"*Which way?*" asks Rusty.

I scan the embankment. "*If we follow the river to the right, we'll make it back to the sewer.*"

"*That's the wrong direction,*" argues Rusty.

"*Do you have any better ideas?*"

Rusty pauses for a moment, then he grins. "*Yes.*"

He suddenly runs across the road towards a large signpost. It's pointing left and says STATION in large black lettering.

We must have gone round in circles with that traitor, Joe.

It only takes us twenty minutes to reach the square and the strange, doll-filled clock is just creaking into action. As the final two dolls trundle out on their toy ghost train, the hour chimes. It's eleven o'clock, which means we have seven hours left until the sun rises and we lose Mum and Dad for ever.

We break into a run.

12

Agents 666 and 667 are waiting for us at the station. They whir their wings furiously at us like they're telling us off.

"*Buzz off,*" I snap. "*It's not our fault we lost you. We got attacked by Death Shadows. What's your excuse?*"

The bigger fly, Agent 666, buzzes something which sounds like the fly equivalent of blowing a raspberry.

Rusty would usually laugh at something like this, but he just lowers his head and summons the train using Malachi's whistle.

Somewhere in the darkness, further

down the track, the ghost train whistles an acknowledgement.

Even though I'm see-through, my body is heavy and tired. There's so much that we have to get right to be able to save our parents. One look at Rusty tells me he's feeling the same. It's a twin thing. Somehow, we've got to snap out of it. Time for the reassuring big sister routine (I was born a full twenty-eight minutes before him).

I tap my brother on the arm. "*All we've got to do is find some stupid stone and then everything is going to be okay.*"

"*Is it? We came here to save Mum and Dad and now we're leaving without them.*"

"*I was trying to cheer you up,*" I say huffily.

"*Try harder.*"

I want to thump him, but I'm playing the part of the mature big sister.

"*At least there's no sign of that horrible, spitting—*"

I groan as a rumpled figure emerges from the office at the end of the main building. It's the ticket collector, spittle dangling from his chin.

We tense, but he simply raises his hand and waves us off with a sly smile. He's got what he wanted: rid of us.

The train roars into the station. This time we are ready, and we brace ourselves so we aren't knocked flying. Rusty blows the whistle for it to leave as we jump aboard. It's oddly normal to be back on this see-through train. That might go down as one of my weirdest thoughts ever.

"*How do we get to Hollow Hills Cemetery?*" asks Rusty.

"*Malachi said there were only three stops: Necropolis Station, Hollow Hills and Necropolis City,*" I say.

As if to confirm this, Agents 666 and 667 whir their wings excitedly. The larger fly – the one that seems to be in charge – taps his agreement with a front leg.

Our destination is one less thing to worry about. I flop back onto a see-through seat and will myself to take a break. I'm exhausted, but my brain is racing.

"*Tell me about the barriers between worlds again.*"

"*Well, ghosts and Battle Beast have a lot in common.*"

I nod encouragingly.

"*Sunrise, sunset and midnight are the times of day when the barrier between the living and the dead is at its thinnest and the forces of darkness are strongest. They are the points of no return. We had until sunset to defeat the Cinderman. With Hell Mary in Necropolis City, it's sunrise,*" says Rusty.

"But the tether thing seems to hold true," I say. "*The Cinderman's tether was his heart and even in Necropolis City ghosts still have a physical tether, which keeps them from moving on. Hell Mary holding the circus performers captive by keeping their teeth is just plain nasty.*"

Rusty rubs his hands on his jeans as if the thought of it needs wiping away. "*Do you think all tethers are human remains?*"

I pause, letting the idea sink in. "*Gross, but possible. It all adds up.*"

"*You know that Seba's tooth is probably his tether. That's why Hell Mary wants it back in that revolting ring.*"

"*The question is, why isn't it still in the ring?*"

"*Maybe it got lost.*" Rusty looks at me and blinks several times.

"*What?*" I say, sitting up straighter, ready to run if he says there's something behind me.

"*Don't take this as a compliment, but you're looking better the further we get from Necropolis City,*" says Rusty.

I smile as I look down to see the colour starting to return to my hands.

"*You too,*" I say. "*Less grey and see-through.*"

"*That's one of the nicest things you could say to me right now.*" Rusty's stomach grumbles. "*That and 'Here's the biggest triple cheese pizza in the world all for you.'*"

The train starts to slow, and we both rush to the window as it bursts out of the darkness and into a starry night. Beyond spike-topped metal railings, a moonlit graveyard stretches ahead of us. It's dotted with tall trees, statues and shadowy monuments. I'm sure I can spot at least two chapels of rest.

Our first stop might be a cemetery, but at least we're back in the land of the living.

"*It's huge!*" says Rusty. "*How are we ever going to find Seba's grave?*"

Reluctantly – I really don't want to touch it – I reach into my pocket and pull out the empty ring Hell Mary gave me.

"*We've got this,*" I say, eyeing it warily.

The train stops and we get off, but Agents 666 and 667 stay on board.

The biggest fly taps out the word "M–A–L–A–C–H–I" on the window.

He's part of them and they are part of him. Maybe they can't be separated for too long. I don't really understand how it works or why he's different from other ghosts, but there's so much that doesn't make sense to me – what's one more thing? I find myself wishing, yet again, that our Spooksmith ancestors had left us some kind of guide. Rusty and I keep a note of everything we learn. We have a whole casebook on the Cinderman and, if we survive this next investigation, we'll put one together on Hell Mary too.

The train departs in a whoosh of steam and smoke, leaving Rusty and me at Hollow Hills Station. The building beside us is in the same style as the station in Necropolis City. It's smaller, but it has a funny pointy roof and clock tower and three separate entrances for the three different classes of passengers. And one for the coffins. The Victorians were obviously obsessed with telling the time and ranking everyone. A bit like school...

An ugly modern red-brick extension has been added to the side of the old building. Next to it is something my stomach has been dreaming about.

"Is that a vending machine?"

To free up my hands, I shove the ring onto the index finger of my right hand and we both run for the shining beacon of junk food. Racks of treats are suspended just out of reach behind thick glass. Our stomachs rumble like they're talking to the snacks inside.

"Got any change?" I ask. I wish I hadn't spent everything on a stuffed tiger and pyjamas in the zoo gift shop followed by lavender air freshener and seasoning in Westminster Bridge Road.

Rusty grins and produces several pound coins from his jeans pockets. "Emergency stash," he says.

Rusty treats us to two packets of crisps, four chocolate bars and a fizzy drink each.

Mum would freak at the sugar and salt content of our

snack, but I know she only fusses about our diet because she cares. If eating something green would bring our parents back, I'd do it in a heartbeat. But it won't. So, I stuff the crisps and chocolate in, trying to fill the emptiness that only saving Mum and Dad can fill.

In the time it takes to walk through the station into the graveyard, we gobble everything.

"That must be a record," says Rusty, giving a loud burp. "I feel waaay better."

"You sound better too," I add. The weak, echoey note to our voices has gone now we're back where we belong.

Rusty scrunches up his fizzy drink can and tosses it in the bin beside the cemetery entrance. There's a loud squeak and several rats scatter from the bin and scurry towards a tall bank of weeds at lightning speed. I swear the last one pauses before it disappears into them – a little grey rat with a white patch over one eye and a pink nose and tail – and then it's gone.

"Did you see that?" I ask.

"Yeah," says Rusty. "Full on infestation, but that's not the weirdest thing I've seen in the last second."

Rusty's staring at me oddly.

"What?"

"The ring Hell Mary gave you… It's shining."

I flip my hand over. The ring is emitting a weird creepy glow as though it's lit from beneath. It's the same sort of light the street lights give off in Necropolis City.

"Hell Mary said the ring would lead us to Seba..."

"Maybe the closer we get to Seba, the more it glows," says Rusty.

Hurriedly, we shove our rubbish in the bin next to the map of the graveyard. This place is even bigger than I thought, with different woodlands, glades and chapels for different faiths, different parishes, and different nationalities. It's like a mini world.

Rusty groans. "It's almost a hundred acres. It could take all night just to walk round it."

"Then we'd better get started," I say.

Three gravel paths stretch ahead of us into the darkness.

"Pick one," I say.

Rusty points and we take the path to the left, skirting the edge of the graveyard beside the railway line. I hold my ring-bearing hand out ahead of me. The light from it waxes and wanes with every twist and turn in the path. A couple of times it goes out completely.

"The ring loses its glow when I'm facing the opposite way to Seba's grave," I say, coming to a stop and turning one hundred and eighty degrees to prove my point.

The glow from the ring blinks out.

"Then we follow the light," says Rusty.

We weave deeper into the graveyard, off the path, following the glow of the ring. Our feet sink into damp mossy ground and thick beds of pine needles, releasing earthy smells of soil and sap.

There's a hoot and Rusty jumps a mile.

"It's only an owl," I say. "This place must be crawling with wildlife."

As if in answer, there's a scurrying of feet and a glint of shining eyes. I smile. We're definitely not alone, but I'm not afraid. Those feet and eyes belonged to a rat, and I can hear the distant screech-bark of badgers at play. I've also just stepped over some muntjac deer droppings. It's all reassuringly normal and makes me realize how soulless Necropolis City felt without animals. I almost acknowledge a pang of sympathy for Joe. Until I remind myself that he betrayed us.

We reach the top end of the graveyard. Hell Mary's ring is glowing at its brightest, lighting up my whole hand. We search all the graves nearby, from simple crosses to ornate statue-covered graves and huge gated monuments. None of them bear the name *Seba Smiles*.

"He's not here," says Rusty, panic creeping into his voice.

"It doesn't make any sense," I say. "Every time I move towards the boundary fence the ring glows brighter, but there's nothing over there... The graveyard is in here and Hell Mary said Seba was buried in Hollow Hills Cemetery."

Before I can say any more, Rusty half climbs, half scrambles up the slatted wooden fence lining the boundary and drops down on the other side. The fence is tall. I can just see the top of his head.

Rusty gives a long, low whistle.

Please let that mean he's found something useful.

"You should see this..." he calls.

It doesn't take me long to scramble over the fence after Rusty. We're on a patch of scrubland. Orange street lights blink in the distance through the branches of leafless trees, but people and their busy lives suddenly feel very far away. This place – whatever it is – has a melancholy, forgotten energy that I didn't get from the graveyard. The grass is long, and it's threaded with weeds and patches of brambles. It's clear that no one has been here for a very long time.

The ring on my finger seems excited. It's radiating light like a beacon, illuminating something on the floor ahead, hidden by the long grass. I kneel and pull the vegetation away. It's a tiny headstone with the name *Cherry* and underneath that *Beloved friend* carved into the weather-beaten stone.

"There's another one here," says Rusty. He peels a clump of moss back to reveal a similar stone, this time with the name *Prince*.

We move through the field, uncovering more stones. Now we know what to look for, we can see hundreds of them, all dotted around with names like *Dotty*, *Topper* and *Jock*.

"Why are these stones so small and why aren't they in the proper part of the graveyard?" asks Rusty.

I've been asking myself the same questions.

"The names," I say, and it comes to me in a flash. "These are animals' names. This is a pet cemetery. I don't understand why, but Seba must be buried here. Look."

I show him the ring. The gap where the stone – or tooth – should sit is glowing so brightly I can't stare at it directly.

"So, where's the grave?" asks Rusty, still digging through the undergrowth.

I look down at the mound of earth under my feet.

"Rusty," I whisper and step back.

It's unmarked, there's no headstone or cross to show that anyone or anything is buried here, but the ring is ablaze.

Immediately, Rusty hurries over. He picks up an old iron railing and starts to stab it into the ground, loosening the soil until he can lift patches of grass and earth.

I hesitate to join him.

"Don't you think we should make a plan, or at least try to find out more about Seba before we dig him up?" I reason. "What if he's dangerous? What if it's not him?"

"You heard Hell Mary. We have until sunrise and it's already one in the morning. Start digging." He's already created a small pit.

Unlike Rusty, I've been responsible for releasing monsters before. I don't want to do it again without thinking it through.

"What if he's like the Cinderman?" I ask.

Rusty stops digging. He pushes a curly strand of hair out of his eyes, leaving a streak of mud across his forehead. "He's probably just a bag of bones. Stop stressing."

"But what if—"

"Indigo, he can take us to the Show Stone. He's our only chance to get Mum and Dad back."

Their names burn a hole in my heart.

Maybe Rusty's right. Maybe this is the only way...

"I've got something!" yells Rusty.

He's hunched over, brushing soil off something small in the centre of his palm. The moon and stars have disappeared behind a thick bank of clouds as though they can't bear to watch what comes next, but the ring shines on. It's not a nice light though, it somehow drains the colour from everything, and the atmosphere is charged, like just before a storm. Something bad is about to happen.

"Rusty..." I warn, but he's oblivious.

"Look!" he says, getting to his feet.

He thrusts the thing he's dug up towards me.

It's a gold tooth.

I wrinkle my nose, but I know what I've got to do. I hold the ring out for Rusty to return the tooth to the setting – there's no way I'm touching it – just as the moon comes out from behind a cloud. Its silvery beams hit the gold tooth and there's a crack of thunder and a bright flash. I turn away, just for a second. When I turn back around, a ginormous clown with blood-red lips is grinning down at us.

13

The clown widens his smile as he sees the horror on both our faces. He leans forward, takes the gold tooth from Rusty's quivering outstretched hand and somehow fixes it back in his ghostly mouth.

"*Scream for Seba, children.*"

His voice is croaky, as though it hasn't been used in a long time, and it's filled with menace. It and his face are totally at odds with his "fun" red-and-white stripy all-in-one and giant flower-decorated shoes. And he knows it. He dances a little jig around Rusty. The overall effect is horrific, like watching a cat toy with a bird before biting its head off.

Rusty is pale and his eyes are wide as though he can't believe what he is seeing. He makes no attempt to move.

"L-leave him alone." My voice is stuttering and shaky. It's hard to get the words out.

Seba stops dancing and turns to me. He's smiling so hard now I can see the white paint cracking in the lines of his face. The menace is only slightly offset by a tiny, fluffy white ghost dog, which scrambles out of the open grave and starts barking at Seba to be picked up. Other than Malachi's flies, I've never seen a ghostly animal before. I can't stop staring.

"*Who are you, little girl?*" Seba asks me. He scoops up the yapping pup and steps closer, pulling himself up to his full height so that he's towering over me.

My legs quiver, but I stand my ground. Names have power. The Cinderman taught me that. There's no way I'm giving him mine unless I have to.

"Hell Mary sent us," I say, avoiding his question.

That takes the smile off his face. Even the little dog in his arms growls.

"*What does that soul-sucking old bat want?*" says Seba, in a voice filled with venom.

That wasn't the reaction I was expecting. My eyes meet Rusty's, and he frowns, just as confused as I am.

"Sh-she called you her soulmate," says Rusty. "She said to tell you that she forgives you."

Seba gives a laugh that's sharp enough to cut glass. *"She called me her soulmate, and she forgives me?"* he hisses, as though he can't believe what he's hearing.

"She said you would help us find her Show Stone," I add.

"That cursed thing," he says, curling his top lip. He's not the only one who's called it cursed – I wonder again what secrets the Stone holds.

"We have to bring it to Hell Mary," says Rusty, panic creeping into his voice. "She's kidnapped our parents. If we don't return it to her in Necropolis City by sunrise they will die."

Seba is giving nothing away. He narrows his eyes. *"How did you find me?"*

"She gave us this ring. She said you'd help," I say, although the possibility of this ghost helping us is looking as likely as a wolf refusing a bite of a nice, tasty rabbit.

Seba taps his gold tooth like he's reassuring himself it's really there.

"Will you help us?" pleads Rusty. "Will you take us to the Show Stone?" He sounds utterly desperate.

There's a moment when a flash of something like pity crosses Seba's face. Then it's gone. His mouth stretches into a forced grin as though he's made a decision.

"*Time to find the Stone,*" he sings in a mock-jaunty way. He tucks the little dog into the large pocket of his all-in-one.

I thought Seba would take more persuading, but this seems to be going our way. I give Rusty a thumbs up for the pleading.

As we move to follow Seba, he gives a sinister little wave.

"*You're not invited. Follow me, and I'll skin you alive.*" He grins and then sets off at a lolloping run.

The words "skin you alive" echo in my head and I'm sure the sky darkens and takes on a more threatening presence... but there's no way we can let our only lead escape.

We give chase. Unfortunately, while Seba leaps through every obstacle and away, Rusty and I are left to scramble over fences, battle our way through undergrowth and run around graves. We're trailing within seconds, and within minutes Seba has disappeared.

"Come back!" I yell, coming to a stop.

"That proves my 'all clowns are evil' theory." Rusty pants, holding his sides.

I kick out at a molehill, sending soil flying. "Seba and Hell Mary are as bad as each other. What are we going to do now? We've got no lead. No one to help us find the Show Stone."

"There's got to be another way," says Rusty.

"What other way?" I snap. "You shouldn't have been so

quick to dig him up – we needed to make a plan. I told you to wait."

Rusty glares at me. "You're not blaming me for this."

"You just couldn't wait for me to think things through first—"

"Stop making it all about you!"

"It's not about me! It's about Mum and Dad!"

We both fall silent as the words "Mum and Dad" echo around the graveyard. What I wouldn't give for a hug from them now. I sit down heavily on a large rock.

"Sorry." I sniff.

Rusty puts his hand on my shoulder. "We should go back to Seba's grave. He's obviously a powerful ghost – definitely a Category Three, maybe even a Four. Let's see if he's left us any clues that might help us track him and the Show Stone down."

I open my mouth to take charge.

"Just for once, Indigo, let me take the lead."

I'm always the leader and it's weird not to argue with him about it. But it's the right thing to do, like when I let Dad take my hand at Waterloo Station. The thought of Dad makes the graveyard seem even darker and lonelier. I stick close to Rusty, following him back to the pet cemetery.

"I don't think Hell Mary and Seba are 'soulmates'," says

Rusty as we walk. "Cellmates, maybe. He hates her."

"He felt the same about the Show Stone as the other performers though. He called it cursed."

"But cursed by who, or what?" asks Rusty.

There's a catlike screech behind us, followed by a yowl and the chatter of birds.

We've just clambered back over the fence into the pet cemetery when chilled air wraps around my ankles. It's the kind of cold that only comes when ghosts are near, or if you get a snowball down the back of your neck.

"Rusty?" I whisper.

"Yeah, I feel it."

And then we see it. And by *it*, I mean *them*...

Around fifty ghostly eyes are fixed on us.

They aren't human.

Several cats, a large pack of dogs, at least four mice, two budgies, one rat, a snake and a tortoise all peer out from the undergrowth.

"I suppose we should have expected animal visitors in a pet cemetery," says Rusty, but his tone of voice tells me he is as surprised as I am.

"Why are we seeing animal ghosts now and not before? What's different about these ones?" I say, approaching a scruffy-looking grey rat with a half-chewed-off ear and a white patch over one eye. I hold out my hand and he sniffs it, chilling it to the bone with his ghostly breath.

"They know we can see them. Maybe they want our help," says Rusty, as two ghostly cats curl around and then half disappear into his legs.

There's a piece of roughly cut slate stuck in the ground behind the ghost rat. Wobbly and misspelled words are carved into the face:

TROY
BELOVD COMPANYON AND LOYLE FREND
DIED 1860

And suddenly I understand.

"Maybe wild animals move on because they have nothing tying them to this world, but creatures that have become companions – like these animals – can't or don't want to move on without their human," I add. "Didn't Joe say his rat was called Troy?"

Rusty nods. "Maybe these pets' tethers are their humans, and they can't reconnect with them because they're all in Necropolis City and Necropolis City doesn't allow animals—"

"—so they're all stuck here, waiting," I say, pity choking my words.

Poor Joe and Troy. I push away the sadness and let my temper boil at the injustice.

"Just wait until I see that Malachi Innspectre again! He says he makes the rules so I'm going to tell him where he can shove them!"

All the animals have crept closer now and I sit down beside them. They know that unlike other living humans, we can see them. Some of them must have spent over one hundred and fifty years being ignored and now they are eager for attention. A terrier drops a ghostly bone in my lap for me to throw and the budgies hop closer, chirping.

"Indigo, I know you love animals, and I want to help them too, but we've got a clown to catch and a Show Stone to find."

Rusty's right. I get up off the ground and brush myself down, trying to ignore the needy stares from the animals.

"We'll make this right. I promise," I tell them.

"First things first – we managed to figure out who the Cinderman was, so how hard can it be to track down a clown and a cursed crystal ball? What do we know so far?" says Rusty.

"Amira said the Circus of Shadows used to be called the Starlight Circus," I say.

"And she talked about it being in a Hippo-something—"

"Hippodrome," I say, rolling my eyes.

"What's that?"

"Er...I dunno." Sheepishly, I take my phone out of my pocket. The battery is registering at one per cent. Why did I take so many photos at the zoo this morning? I quickly type "hippodrome" into the search bar and the battery dies.

Rusty takes over, using his own phone. "One: a theatre or concert hall. Two: (in ancient Greece or Rome) a course for chariot or horse races."

"Look up anywhere in London that has Hippodrome or Starlight in the name."

Rusty taps away. "There's Happy Hippos Whacky Warehouse, Hippy Dippy's Ice Creams, some show called *Starlight Express*... Oh, hang on, there's a Starlight Circus Bar coming up."

"Where is it?" I try to peer at the screen, but Rusty snatches it away.

"I can't type with you sticking your nose in."

"Type quicker then." I tap my foot.

Rusty lowers the phone with a smug smile plastered across his face.

"Out with it!"

"The Starlight Circus Bar just so happens to be in the Hippodrome Hotel."

"Brilliant! Where is it?"

"You'll never guess..."

Rusty could get a GCSE in being annoying.

"Just spit it out!"

"Westminster Bridge Road."

"But that's where—"

Rusty grins. "It's the other end of the road to Necropolis Station, but glad to see you're paying attention."

"Are you sure?"

"Pretty sure." He shows me photographs of the bar on the website. It's full of circus memorabilia from wooden fairground horses on top of the booths, to signs, posters, funfair mirrors, masks and costumes. And on a stand, at the back of the bar, behind a metal cage, is a crystal ball.

Somewhere in the distance a clock chimes one in the morning and I shiver. Five hours to save Mum and Dad.

"Let's get back on that train and beat Seba to it."

14

We race back to the railway station at Hollow Hills, flopping down inside the see-through train as it puffs out of the station.

"The last time I ran that hard was when Battle Beast dropped its Razorspine Revival limited edition set and I was at the beach," Rusty says, panting.

"Why is everything always a race against time?" I ask. My mouth is drier than a box of crackers. I wish I'd kept some of my drink from earlier.

"Technically, this is a race against Seba,"

Rusty corrects me. "If he beats us to that Stone, I doubt he's going to hand it over."

There's a scuttling from underneath the seat and a pointy face with a pink nose emerges. It's a grey rat with a white patch over one eye. I'm pretty sure it's the one we saw from the bin earlier: an actual live rodent as opposed to a ghostly one. How and why is it on a ghost train?

"Is it me or is that rat staring at me?" says Rusty.

The rat is sitting up on its haunches, head cocked to one side, gazing up at Rusty with adoration. It's most definitely not normal street rat behaviour.

Another rat squeaks and pushes its face up between the seats. It has the same markings as the rat under the seat, but this one is see-through and ghostly.

"Is that Troy?" I ask.

Troy squeaks as if in answer.

"He must have followed us," says Rusty.

"And brought along a friend."

"Do ghost rats have live rat friends?" says Rusty.

I stare between the two rats. "They look quite alike. Maybe they're related."

"Well, I'm not related to them, so why is that one staring at me?" asks Rusty, pointing at the live rat with the pink nose.

"It's got a crush on you," I say. "Try staring back, that should frighten it away."

Rusty gives the rat the full-on evil eye.

"Nothing," says Rusty. "It's not even flinching under the beam of my most stinky glare and I'm giving it all I've got."

"Weird," I say, peering at it.

The rat is small – for a rat – about the length of my size fives, tail included. Its fur is light grey, and its little paws, tail and nose are pale pink. One eye is surrounded by a white patch and both eyes are black and bright. Its white whiskers are quivering in anticipation of something.

Rusty tries to shoo it away, but it just squeaks at him.

"I think you're right about the crush. This rat loves me," he says. "It can't get enough."

"What if..." I wonder out loud. "No... Maybe...?"

"Spit it out before this rodent asks me to marry it!"

I slide off my seat and onto the floor, but the rat keeps staring at Rusty. It's gazing at him in the same sort of way Phrank looks at me when he's in an especially good mood.

"Don't freak out," I say. "But what if this rat is your Phrank?"

"My what?" he says.

"Grandpa said Spooksmiths often have an animal sidekick, and you don't have one yet. Phrank tolerates you, but he's definitely more mine than yours."

"But why is my sidekick showing up now?" asks Rusty.

"Maybe he senses we need all the help we can get," I say.

Rusty eyes the rat warily. "I was hoping for a scarier sidekick, like a bear or a wolf. Or a hybrid of the two. How do I know we're connected?" he asks.

I shrug. "There's no Spooksmith rule book, but with Phrank I just knew. Try feeding him something."

Rusty rummages in his pocket and produces a sliver of hairy biscuit.

"What if he bites my fingers off and gives me rabies?"

"Then you'll know he's not your animal sidekick."

Cautiously, Rusty approaches the rat. He kneels and holds out his left hand, bearing the crumbs as though they are a sacrifice. "If it chows down on my left, I can still Battle Beast with my right. Do your worst, tiny fiend."

The rat gives a squeak of glee and leaps onto his hand, nibbling gently at the pocket snacks.

I watch Rusty's expression change from scrunched up and nervous to wide-eyed wonder. When the rat finishes eating, he runs up Rusty's arm and sits on his shoulder. Rusty stands up. He's never really been an animal person – unlike me – but his face is taking on that proud and excited look he gets when he's saved up enough money to buy a new Battle Beast set.

"Let me introduce you to my animal sidekick, Fangor

Death Render. Or Fang for short," says Rusty, grinning like a kid at Christmas.

Fang squeaks something and Rusty nods. Oh, please don't tell me my brother thinks he can speak rat. We've got enough problems without him thinking he's suddenly turned into Dr Dolittle.

"You know you can't actually talk to your animal sidekick, right?"

"Yeah." Rusty sniffs. "But we've got an understanding."

It's the same with me and Phrank. We just kind of get each other. And if I don't meet Phrank's expectations, he's quick to peck me back into line. Not to mention the fact that he saved my life when I was investigating the Cinderman in Greyscar Mine. I know he'd help us beat Seba to the Show Stone. I miss him.

"All that rubbish about animals not having souls." I shake my head. "Once we've got that Show Stone and Mum and Dad are safe, we're going to have a word with Malachi."

Rusty, Troy and Fang are now happily sharing a seat.

"Fang could be Troy's great-great-great-great-great-great-great-great-grandson," says Rusty.

"He could," I say, trying not to flinch as the train makes its usual low-key entrance into Necropolis Station – straight through a brick wall.

We disembark, Fang sitting on Rusty's shoulder and Troy trotting alongside. Both of us are on high alert for any sign of Malachi and his flies, but he doesn't appear, and we don't hang around to look for him.

Two taxis blink by as we hurry down Westminster Bridge Road. There are no people and even the corner shop with the annoying teenager behind the till is in darkness. We cross a small grassy square. On the other side is a grand building. It's five storeys high with a tower and metal dome with a statue of two horses rearing up. *The Hippodrome Hotel and Starlight Circus Bar* is written on it in big gold lettering.

We push our faces up against the glass door. The entrance foyer is huge, the ceiling stretching away to the height of a double-decker bus. A glitzy, glass chandelier hangs in the centre, making the silver-flecked marble floor and fish tank centrepiece sparkle. There's a reception desk to the left with a woman in a smart navy suit behind it. She's tapping something into her computer.

"I'm not sure she's going to let us and a pair of rats in," says Rusty. "Even if one of them is a ghost."

The woman behind the desk takes a phone call and then disappears through a door in the panelling behind her.

"Now," I say.

We slip inside, darting across the foyer. Fang and Troy

lead the way, sniffing the ground as though they can pick up the scent of the Show Stone.

We hurry along a glass corridor lined with palm trees, and take the stairs down, following a brass sign marked *Ballroom* and *Starlight Circus Bar*.

Outside the ballroom are trolleys piled with napkins and plates and uneaten canapés. They must be left over from some fancy party. There are no staff around, which is lucky because Fang leaps onto the pigs in blankets.

Other than the crisps and chocolate at Hollow Hills Station, we've had nothing much to eat since lunch yesterday. We quickly scavenge what we can as we hurry past. Troy watches on, but Fang looks like he's settling in for *Come Dine With Me*. He's dragging a smoked salmon vol-au-vent across the trolley while trying to rat-handle a pork pie.

"Fang, we need to go," says Rusty.

Fang swallows a cheese straw and blinks up at Rusty as though he doesn't understand. I might be about to witness their first official fallout.

"Fang," says Rusty, irritation creeping into his voice. "Come on. We have to beat Seba to the Show Stone."

He picks Fang up – still clinging to a chicken leg – and puts him on the floor.

Fang looks at the chicken leg and then at Rusty and squeaks.

"Okay," says Rusty, rolling his eyes. "I'll put the chicken leg in my pocket for later."

He shoves the half-chewed leg in his pocket – rather him than me – and we all run on.

Ahead is a mirrored door which stretches our reflections, making us all look as long and thin as worms. The sign above it reads: *Starlight Circus Bar*.

I grasp the crystal handle. It's cool to the touch – not just everyday chilly, but ghost cold – and I open the door.

"Mmmm, smells like a breakfast smoothie in here," says Rusty.

He's right. The room is pitch black, but I'm hit by the scent of coconut and banana. I lean around the door and flick several switches. The lights flicker on.

The walls are painted a deep, beetroot red and light bulbs spelling the words "Smile" and "Showtime" decorate the walls. There's a mirrored bar, one end of which is piled with empty glasses, banana skins and flowery cocktail umbrellas.

I point at a large board at the back of the bar advertising cocktails with names like "Lava Flow" and "Dirty Banana".

"That explains the smell," I say.

The bar is surrounded by at least twenty green leather booths with carousel horses standing on the back of them, but I can't see anything that resembles—

"Look," says Rusty, pointing to a marble stand on the left-hand side of the room.

"Is that what I think it is?" I ask.

Black gauzy curtains are draped either side of the stand and on top of it, encased in a spiralled metal cage, is what can only be the Show Stone.

It's quite something. Four spotlights illuminate the Stone from beneath, making it easy to see every detail, even through the metal cage. And the detail that's caught my attention is the blood-red liquid floating in the centre of the Stone.

"Son of Smite!" says Rusty. "That's way worse than in the photo. It's creepier than a busload of clowns. Bags not being the one to carry it."

I shoot him a look.

"The Stone is your Chuckles," he insists. "You carry it."

Chuckles is a ghostly toddler who helped us beat the Cinderman. He insisted on being carried around by Rusty, so I guess, technically, it is my turn.

"Fine," I say, wrinkling my nose at the bloody interior of the Stone.

I'm halfway across the room, weaving around the booths to reach the crystal ball, when a movement catches my eye. My skin turns clammy. It's like my body senses who it is and what's about to happen a split second before it does. So do Fang and Troy. They're both squeaking like crazy.

There's a glint of a gold tooth in a white face and then all the lights go out. I'm plunged into darkness so thick it's like Hell Mary's scratched my eyes out. It's claustrophobic and disorientating. I stumble forwards, determined to beat Seba to the crystal ball.

"Indigo!" yells Rusty.

"Get the Stone!" I yell back.

This can't be happening. Red-hot panic descends. Hands out in front, I feel my way around a table, crying out as I catch my knee on a hard corner. Ghosts can see in the dark. I remember that from when I was trying to outrun the Cinderman in Greyscar Mine. Humans can't, not even if they eat lots of carrots. Not even if they're Spooksmiths.

Rusty's crashing around to my left. He must be going over the top of the booths because I can hear the squeak of trainers on the leather seats and grunts of exertion as he negotiates the carousel horses.

Seba can't beat us to that Stone. We're so close...

Crowing laughter makes my heart lurch, and that lurch turns into free fall when a croaky voice calls out, *"Finders keepers!"*

15

I career towards that croaky voice in the dark but all I find is the light switch. I hit it and the light bulbs crackle back to life.

Rusty is on top of a carousel horse and Fang is beside him. They are both looking down on a humongous ghost clown holding a caged crystal ball.

"*It's mine!*" says Seba.

"No, it isn't," says Rusty, diving off the horse, Fang and Troy by his side.

The little ghost dog is in Seba's pocket, yapping and snarling as Seba dodges them and tries to run through a wall. Immediately, he's jolted backwards. He can't get all the way through it because he's holding a solid object: the Show Stone.

"*Curse you!*" Seba screams with frustration, as the ball flies into the air.

"I've got it!" I yell.

"No, I've got it!" yells Rusty.

"*It's coming with me!*" screeches Seba, hurling banana skins, cocktail umbrellas and a handful of novelty magician's wands at us.

"Ha! It'll take more than a banana skin to stop me!" says Rusty, only to crash to the floor when he trips on his own shoelace.

I dodge the missiles and launch myself forward.

"*Stop them, Bunnykins!*" yells Seba, and the little dog leaps from his pocket.

I burst through Seba's ghostly frame. It's like diving head first into a snowdrift, but I reach the Stone before it hits the floor.

I gasp as my fingers close around it and needles of ice stab my palms. What is this thing made of? I squeal and drop it. The Stone rolls away beneath a booth to where Bunnykins is waiting. He yips with glee.

There's a cry behind me. I check over my shoulder to find Rusty throwing handfuls of salt from behind the bar. Each time he makes a direct hit, ghostly smoke spirals off Seba.

Seba successfully distracted, I dive under the booth. Bunnykins might look like a cute fluffy white dog, but he snaps at me with sharp, ghostly teeth, protecting the Stone. I don't know if a ghost dog can bite but I don't want to test it. I pull my hand away.

Fang and Troy scuttle to my side and launch a two-pronged attack. Fang distracts Bunnykins by baring his teeth and squeaking, while Troy races around and barrels into Bunnykins' side, wrapping ghostly paws around him, rolling him over and out of the way. Now's my chance – I quickly shrug off my coat and wrap it around the Stone.

I emerge from under the booth victorious and Seba starts towards me.

"Don't even think about it," says Rusty, waving a big bottle of lavender cocktail syrup in Seba's direction.

Seba's face falls, face paint crumbling onto his costume. He suddenly looks very old. *"You're making a terrible mistake,"* he croaks.

I pause. All Rusty and I have thought about is finding the Stone so we can get Mum and Dad back, but we haven't really considered why Hell Mary wants it. She said it can show the past and the future, and that it would restore her circus to its former glory, but I think there's even more to it.

"You made a mistake when you decided not to help us," says Rusty.

"*You don't know what you're doing. You don't know what that is,*" says Seba. He sounds more pleading than terrifying now. Bunnykins is back in his arms and he's cuddling the little dog as though someone's life depends on it. What's he playing at? What is the Stone really? I wish Mum was here now. She's good at getting people to talk, thanks to all her counselling courses.

Before I can question him further, raised voices come from the corridor outside the bar. All the noise we've been making obviously hasn't gone unnoticed. Before I can warn Rusty, a woman in a suit two sizes too big bursts into the room. She's followed by two dishevelled male members of staff – one tall, one short. They're rubbing their eyes like they've just woken up.

"What the..." says the woman wearing a lopsided *Manager* badge on her lapel. She takes in the salty, bananary mess all over the floor and her face goes pale. I'm just imagining how much worse it would be if she could actually *see* ghostly Seba, Bunnykins and Troy, when she spots me and Rusty.

Her face goes from white to red and she puffs out her cheeks.

"I don't think she's about to congratulate us on our redecorating skills," says Rusty, already backing away.

"Move!" I shout.

"Give that back, girl, it's private property!" shouts the manager, making a snatch for the Stone.

She misses and Rusty and I take cover behind a booth where Fang and Troy are already hiding.

The two sleepy employees shuffle towards us. The tall one shivers as he brushes close to Seba, who is standing against the wall tapping his giant, clown-shoed foot.

"It's freezing in here," says the tall employee, teeth chattering.

"That'll be the ghost you just stepped into," I say, peering out from behind the booth.

The tall man stops. "Ghost?"

"There's no such thing as ghosts," snaps the manager.

Before my Spooksmith powers kicked in on my twelfth birthday, I used to think the same thing.

The two employees surround Rusty and me.

"Give me that Stone," says the short man.

And I don't know why I do it, as Seba has done nothing to help us so far, but I look at him and mouth the word *please*.

Seba looks as though he's going to refuse, but then a slow smile spreads across his terrifying, cracked face.

"*Hell Mary. Hell Mary. Hell Mary,*" he says into the mirrored glass.

Wonderful. Seba has just made everything worse. I thought he hated Hell Mary, but he obviously hates Rusty and me more.

"Who said that?" squeaks the tall man, spinning around.

Seba is definitely a Category Four ghost. Not only can he handle everyday, solid objects and seemingly travel wherever he pleases, but he can also make live humans hear him.

"Never mind who said it. Who's that?" says the short man.

Hell Mary's veiled reflection has appeared in the mirrored bar.

At first glance, she gets a ten out of ten for creep factor – all billowing black lace, hunched shoulders, jangling necklaces and click-clacking rings. I stare at her for a few seconds. There's something off about her. She's walking back and forth again and again, a mirrored necklace twisting at her throat. It's like she's on a loop. She never makes a move to come out of the mirror and she never turns towards us. It's as though she can't see us.

"*Meet Hell Mary,*" crows Seba.

"Hell Mary!" screams the tall man. "Cover your eyes or she'll scratch them out!"

"*That's one of the old bag's specialities!*" croaks Seba. "*You'd better run before she bursts out of that mirror and gets you!*"

"If this is Seba's idea of help, I don't think we want it," whispers Rusty from our position behind the booth.

I shake my head. "I don't understand it, but I'm not sure it's really her. I don't think she can come out of the mirror. She's just a reflection." Which means Seba did help us after all. Maybe there's more to this terrifying ghost clown than I first thought.

The two hotel employees aren't hanging around to find out if she's a reflection or not. They're too busy trying to back out of the room with their hands over their eyes. They crash into furniture and knock over several glasses.

"Stop it this instant!" snaps the manager. "It's just some silly game these children are playing! They've obviously got something rigged up to the mirror to create that hideous illusion." She turns to the short man. "Carl, get those children. And Frederik, stop talking nonsense about ghosts and call the police."

The Hell Mary in the mirror fades away. Perhaps her reflection can only remain here for so long.

As Carl closes in again, Rusty and I scramble under the closest table. Rusty whispers something to Fang. Fang releases a cacophony of high-pitched squeaks and Troy joins in.

Frederik drops his phone and the manager freezes.

"It's not...is that...?" She points with a finger as Fang pokes his little pink nose out from under the table. "Rat!" she screams.

The manager isn't bothered by one of the most terrifying ghosts of all time, but she is upset about a small, squeaky rodent. I shake my head in disbelief. Some people blow my mind.

Fang squeaks and takes off and Troy joins him, skittering out from beneath the table, claws skidding on the polished wood floor.

"Call the exterminator!" screams the manager.

Frederik and the manager jump up onto a table as the rats bolt for the door. Fang slides beneath it and Troy goes straight through it, and both are away.

I was so sure Fang was Rusty's sidekick. I can't hide the fact that I'm disappointed in him.

"What are we going to do now?" I whisper to Rusty.

"Don't worry about it," says Rusty. "Fang's got this."

I frown.

"Seriously, don't worry." Rusty grins. "If one rat gets her jumping on the table, imagine what's going to happen in three..."

It takes me a moment to notice the distant rumble.

"Two," says Rusty.

The sound builds slowly like a gathering storm. At first, it could be mistaken for a heavy lorry on the road outside, but it keeps getting louder. And louder.

"One," says Rusty as the rumble turns to the thump of feet and the scritch-scratch of hundreds – no, thousands – of tiny claws.

The door to the Starlight Circus Bar shudders.

Thump. Thump. Thump.

Carl backs away from the door.

"What's that?" he asks.

"That's the sound of hundreds of furry bodies hitting the door," I say, finally catching up. I climb out from beneath the table.

"Bodies?" says the tall employee. "What do you mean by 'bodies'."

At that exact moment, the door bursts open to reveal a carpet of hairy rodents. They pour into the room, squeaking and squabbling. Led by Fang and Troy, they surround the manager and her employees and herd them screaming from the room.

Rusty and I sprint after the rats, following them down the corridors and out into the entrance lobby. The hotel workers dive behind the reception desk, crying in fear. Frederik calls out for his mummy. Time to make our escape.

16

We tumble out of the hotel and onto a deserted street. Sirens wail in the distance.

"The manager called the police! Quick!" shouts Rusty.

The rat pack disappear down the nearest drain, apart from Fang and Troy. They sprint with us to Necropolis Station. Interestingly, Seba follows too with Bunnykins in his pocket. He helped us back there, but I'm still wary of him. Rusty is obviously having the same thoughts. He stays close, ready to defend me and the Stone, salt at the ready.

It's not until we burst through the barred gate and reach the platform that I realize our little group isn't alone. Behind me is a ghostly troupe of clowns, a teenage boy as thin as a toothpick, the oldest lady I've ever seen, plus a spooky girl with arm muscles bigger than my head. And they are all staring at the Show Stone.

I freeze. It's like the time I got stage fright on the opening night of the Year Five play. I couldn't remember my lines then, and I can't think of what to say now. I'm a Spooksmith but the desperate way this lot are looking at me is making my nerves twang like a badly played violin.

"*I am Hercules Helen,*" says the strong-looking girl, flexing her muscles. "*And that Stone belongs to us.*"

Rusty steps between me and the ghosts, brandishing a handful of salt. "Back off!" he shouts.

The old lady totters forward next. "*I'm called Blade and we're asking you nicely to give us back our Stone.*"

"Blade?" Rusty sniggers. "Seriously? You look more like a Doris."

Blade flicks open her long coat with surprising speed. She reveals a vest covered with straps and pockets; each one holds a glinting, ghostly knife.

"*We don't want any trouble,*" says Blade, reaching for a knife in a way that says trouble is her middle name.

The clowns gather behind her holding custard pies ready for throwing.

I'm getting the feeling that this isn't going to be a fair fight.

"*Enough,*" says Seba, and Bunnykins growls his agreement. "*I swore to protect these ghosts from Hell Mary, and I will do everything in my power to fulfil my oath but fighting each other won't get us anywhere.*"

Maybe Seba isn't the bad guy we thought he was. Or maybe he's bluffing...

"Why do you need to protect them from Hell Mary?" I ask. "What's so important about this Stone?"

"*You have my tether,*" says the thin boy.

I frown.

"*You don't only have Mac's tether, you've got mine too,*" says Blade.

My blood runs cold as a chorus of, "*And mine*", "*And mine*" goes up from all the other performers.

I shake my head, unwilling to believe it. How can I hand the Stone to Hell Mary if this is true; if it's their tether? A ghost's tether is what keeps a supernatural being stuck in one place – that and unfinished business – but tethers are usually human remains like the Cinderman's heart and Seba's tooth. How can something human be inside a ball of glass?

"You're wrong," I say, wrapping my coat more tightly around it.

Seba scoffs. "*You're the one who's wrong. Tell her—*"

The station clock interrupts him by chiming the hour: three in the morning. My chest tightens. We can't stand around chit-chatting. We're running out of time.

"Hell Mary has kidnapped our parents," says Rusty, still brandishing the salt as a warning. "If we don't deliver this Stone to her in three hours, she's going to let them die."

The performers all start talking at once.

"*I don't want to go back to Hell Mary,*" says Mac.

"*We can't let people die because of us,*" argues Blade.

"*It's too much to ask,*" says one of the clowns.

"*Blade's right and you know it,*" says Hercules Helen, coming to the old lady's defence. "*We're already dead. What's the worst Hell Mary can do to us?*"

"*You know what she's like. She'll make us suffer for eternity,*" says Mac.

I don't want these ghosts to suffer but I don't want to lose my parents either. Maybe, if we work together, we can save everyone.

"We've beaten a Category Five ghost before," I say. "Rusty and I aren't just ordinary kids. We're Spooksmiths. We beat the Cinderman. We can help you defeat Hell Mary."

Rusty nods his agreement.

Seba looks us up and down as though he's deciding whether to believe us.

"*I call a ghostly meeting,*" announces Blade.

The ghosts form a huddle and whisper amongst themselves, but there doesn't seem to be an urgency to their discussion. I tap my foot until Rusty tells me to stop.

After a few minutes, the ghosts break apart.

"*We've reached a decision,*" says Seba. "*The performers have agreed to accompany you on the train so that they can share their story. Once you know the truth about the Stone, it is up to you to decide if you can take on someone as strong and as evil as Hell Mary.*"

"Agreed," I say.

"Sounds good," says Rusty.

Rusty blows the whistle and then darts across to the opposite platform. He rummages through the London Zoo and Battle Beast Universe bags we left there earlier.

"What are you doing?!" I shout, holding onto a pillar to make sure I'm not knocked over by the force of the train's arrival.

"Artefacts for the ferryman!" he replies.

He sprints back just in time to catch the train. We board it along with the ghosts, and the train leaves the station. I wonder briefly where Malachi is, but the thought disappears as we charge through the wall.

"*Let us begin,*" says Seba.

The Stone seems to grow colder in my hands at his words. It also feels heavier, as though it's trying to communicate the weight of its secrets.

"*Once upon a time, there was a place of wonder called the Starlight Circus,*" says Blade. "*There were acrobats and clowns, illusionists and jugglers, contortionists and knife throwers. There were animal acts and music and laughter. All were welcome.*"

The train rattles through the darkness as she talks, and all the performers gather around to listen. Fang and Troy huddle in closer too.

Seba takes over. "*On the 31st of October 1856, I left the circus for a single evening to marry my beloved, Mary. When we returned as man and wife, the circus was burning. Lightning had struck the Hippodrome.*"

"*Some of the performers escaped but the ghosts you see here all perished,*" says Mac.

"*The fire was so hot, it turned a patch of the sandy, bloody floor into a ball of lightning glass,*" says Hercules Helen. Her eyes become cloudy as she talks, and Mac puts a thin arm around her.

All eyes are on me and the Show Stone. The icy cold

radiating from it is burning through the metal cage surrounding it and the material of my coat. My hands shake as the realization of what I'm really holding dawns on me.

"The Show Stone is made from that lightning glass." I whisper the words, as if the truth is too ugly to say aloud. I unwrap it and the red liquid inside it swirls angrily.

"*Our blood is our tether,*" says Mac.

"*And it's in that Stone,*" says the muscly girl.

"But that's horrible!" I say, nearly losing my grip on it.

Seba has dropped the menacing act and his face crumples as he speaks. "*My Mary picked up the glass, promising to bury it in memory of our fallen friends, but from the moment she touched it, I lost her.*"

"*Our ghostly powers were fused into the glass and she created a Show Stone from it,*" explains Mac. "*She used it to become the greatest seer in the world, while we were left weak and helpless ghosts, tethered to the glass.*"

"*Kings and queens paid her small fortunes to tell their futures and to speak to their dead loved ones,*" says Hercules Helen. "*But she also knew their deepest, darkest secrets.*"

"So what happened?" asks Rusty.

"*She started to manipulate people, threatening to reveal their secrets if they didn't do as she asked. She also meddled more and more with the dead side,*" explains Blade.

"*When I died of old age, I couldn't escape her. She had my tooth, my tether,*" explained Seba. "*She became known as Hell Mary and the kings and queens who used to ask for her became scared and begged her to stay away. She was shunned by society and died twisted, bitter and alone.*"

Rusty has gone pale, and a queasiness is churning inside my belly. Hell Mary is even worse than we thought, but there's one thing I'm not getting.

"Why didn't Hell Mary remain here with the Show Stone when she died? The Cinderman haunted our world. Why did Hell Mary go to Necropolis City?"

Seba gives a small smile. "*Someone may have talked her into believing the Show Stone was already on the other side. It was my greatest trick.*"

The clowns smile at him and Blade pats him on the shoulder. It hits me that they are a unit, a family, just as close as Rusty, Mum, Dad and me.

"*In reality, the Show Stone was lost,*" says Seba. "*Stolen the day Hell Mary died by someone who couldn't access its power. It turned up at an auction years later, bought as a trinket by the owners of the newly created Hippodrome Hotel, which was built on the site of—*"

"—the burned-down Hippodrome," guesses Rusty.

"*Correct,*" says Blade. "*It was serendipity. The owners just thought they were buying an old crystal ball; they didn't know they were bringing it home to the place it was created."*

"*We were happy haunting the hotel,*" says Mac, throwing his voice so that it sounds much further away one second and then very close the next. "*That trick used to give guests the heebie-jeebies.*"

Mac's right. Without being able to see him, that floating voice would be properly creepy.

"*Nothing like the sound of a knife whistling through the air to get annoying guests out of* my *suite,*" adds Blade, stroking a short-bladed knife at her side.

"*Ghostly giggles make the world go round,*" says one of the clowns.

"But what about you?" I ask, turning to Seba. "How did you end up in a pet cemetery?"

"*Bunnykins was buried there,*" says Seba. He pets the fluffy little white dog, cooing over it using a baby voice. "*When I died, I wished to be buried with him, but Hell Mary put my remains in the main cemetery. There was nothing I could do, I was a ghost, and I was bound to go where she wanted because she had my tooth tether. Until suddenly she didn't...*"

"You tricked her," says Rusty.

Seba raises his painted-on eyebrows. "*When Hell Mary died and I persuaded her ghost to set foot on that train, she had no reason to believe that she didn't have my tether."* Seba grinned. *"But I'd prised the tooth from her ring the day before. She had so many tooth rings she didn't notice I'd replaced it with a pebble. With no power over me, she could only scream as I waved her off from the station platform. I was free to join my true beloved: Bunnykins. We've been haunting the graveyard together ever since."*

My eyes meet Rusty's. If Hell Mary can be tricked, then maybe she can be beaten.

"If we give Hell Mary the Show Stone, we're betraying everyone here," I say. "If we don't give her the Show Stone, we're killing Mum and Dad."

Rusty shuts his eyes and rubs his head. It's like he's trying to massage some thoughts into that empty space on top of his neck.

When he opens his eyes, his hair is sticking out all over the place, but he's grinning like he's just won a Battle Beast championship.

"I've got an idea that might mean we all win," says Rusty. "Well, everyone but Hell Mary anyway."

"I'm listening," I say.

"I'm all smiles," says Seba.

17

Rusty's plan involves us pulling off the perfect double-cross, all working together, live humans and ghosts, side by side just like when we took down the Cinderman.

Phase one involves giving the Show Stone to Hell Mary and rescuing Mum and Dad.

Phase two is about stealing the Show Stone right back.

The scheme is intricate and involves A LOT of Battle Beast terminology, most of which only Rusty understands. But he seems sure of it. What can go wrong?

The train pulls into Necropolis City and Seba hugs Bunnykins to him as he spots the sign where we disembark.

"No pets. No live humans. No returns." He grins. "We seem to have broken every single rule."

"*Rules are made to be broken,*" says Rusty. "*Especially if you're a Spooksmith.*"

Hercules Helen is flexing her muscles, which seem to have expanded, Mac is solid and less skeletal, the clowns are skipping and even Blade has got a spring in her ancient step. Unfortunately, I've never felt so tired and seeing Rusty dragging his heels tells me he's burnt out too.

Seba looks at us and frowns. "You two are disappearing."

I glance down at my see-through hands clasped around the Show Stone. I grit my teeth.

"*We'll survive,*" I say, my voice all echoey again.

The ghostly ticket collector strides out from his ticket office, waving his ticket book and yelling about, "Unauthorized access!"

Seba runs towards him, slapping his huge clown shoes against the ground like wet fish. The other clowns join him, ghostly custard pies at the ready.

The ghostly ticket collector screams and runs back inside his office.

At any other time, it would have been hilarious, but the Show Stone is pulling my mood down. It's still wrapped in my coat, but coldness and sadness radiate off it. To add to that, worries about whether our plan will work and if Mum and Dad will be okay are chewing away at me like a dog gnawing a bone.

As though Rusty can tell my thoughts are spiralling, he nudges me.

"*We're in this together,*" he whispers.

Without Rusty, I don't know what I'd do. I stay close to him, glad I'm not alone, reminding myself that every step we take is a step closer to saving Mum and Dad.

We make our way across the city to Hell Mary's circus. By the time we arrive at the gloomy-looking big top, my arms are aching, my hands are frozen, and anxiety is making me question every step.

Somewhere in the distance, a clock chimes four in the morning. We've got two hours to find Mum and Dad and get out of here.

The wind picks up, whistling through the buildings and barrelling over the barren and muddy fairground. Torn patches of the stripy tent slap miserably against the sides as though they're waving us in.

"*Stay hidden,*" Rusty whispers to Fang and Troy.

They both squeak and burrow further into the pockets of Rusty's coat.

As soon as we enter the ring, the dark torches flare to life.

"Showtime," mutters Seba, his white face paint crumbling further. "I hope you know what you're doing."

The ghosts we met earlier, Amit and Amira, Ray, the jugglers and the contortionist, are in the ringside seats. They jump up as they see us and their former workmates, but then the darkness at the back of the tent shifts and they shrink back as Hell Mary steps into the ring and into the light.

She moves towards us, face veiled, bone necklaces and teeth rings click-clacking together. She sounds like a walking skeleton.

"I have waited so long for this moment." Her rasping voice cuts through the moaning of the wind and the rustling of the tent.

"*Make sure she tells you where Mum and Dad are first,*" warns Rusty.

"*For sure,*" I say.

I uncover the Show Stone and hold it up with both hands for her to see.

"*It's yours,*" I say, hating my voice for being small and weak and needy. "*In exchange for our parents.*"

Hell Mary's looming frame covers the space between us in

four long strides. I gasp as she snatches it from me. She's so quick I don't have time to think about resisting.

She stares into the Stone. Through the gaps in the metal cage surrounding it, I can see red ribbons of blood bashing at the glass to get out.

"It's mine!" She laughs, twirling around with it like some sort of bad ballerina. "My circus is complete!"

The performers shrink back from her as she cackles.

"*Our parents...where are they?*" says Rusty, but she ignores him.

"I forgive you, my love," says Hell Mary, looking at Seba. "Now we can be together for all eternity."

Seba curls his lip.

"I said I forgive you," hisses Hell Mary. It's less like an apology and more like an order. "With you at my side, we can build this circus back up to its former glory. Show me your love and undying devotion."

"You're not having my love or devotion," snarls Seba. "I'm not here for you. I'm here for them." He points to the performers.

Hell Mary takes a step back and even though she's veiled I'm sure I can see surprise flicker across her shadowy face.

"But we are man and wife."

"Ha! More like clown and monster."

Hell Mary gasps like she's amazed he could possibly make a joke of their union. It's like she imagines she's a great catch despite all the theft, mirror hopping, scratching out eyes, kidnapping and soul-stealing.

"I had no choice but to leave you when you took advantage of the deceased and became obsessed with the Stone," says Seba.

"You were never willing to do what it took to become great!"

"You call this 'great'?" sneers Seba.

"*This is seriously awkward,*" Rusty whispers into my ear.

Despite everything, I snigger, which with the benefit of hindsight, is a mistake.

Hell Mary wheels on me.

"You and your brother have expended your usefulness."

"*Just give us back our parents and we'll happily go,*" I say.

Hell Mary tilts her head. I can tell she's smiling beneath that creepy veil.

"I can't leave you running around alive. Spooksmiths are an abomination. You should not exist."

I take a step back. It's becoming painfully clear that Hell Mary never intended to let us or our parents go free.

"*What do you think you know about us?*" I ask.

"I know that your ancestors meddled with something that did not concern them."

"*Like you with that Show Stone,*" says Rusty.

Hell Mary bristles, but Seba snorts with laughter.

"They've got you there, my love," he crows.

She places the Show Stone into a large sack-like bag and hooks it over her shoulder. Then she strides across the tent and unclips one of the canvas sides. A patch of seething darkness ripples at the far edges of the fairground – Death Shadows.

Hell Mary grins. "I could alert them to your presence with a single word."

Fear swallows all of my bravado and I find myself taking hold of Rusty's hand.

"*This isn't how it was supposed to go,*" whispers Rusty.

Even Seba's face pales. "Mary, they're just stinking children. They've given you what you wanted. Let them go."

I'm not keen on the "stinking" but I know he's trying to help.

"Oh, I'll let them go all right." She cackles. "Straight to their deaths. They've only got a few hours left before their parents are done for anyway. No living human can survive here for long."

Seba turns to me. "Get out of here!"

"*We're not leaving without our parents,*" I argue.

"*Not without Mum and Dad,*" agrees Rusty.

My brother quivers beside me as a howl goes up from the Death Shadows.

"Let them go," says Seba. "For me."

"You called me a monster," hisses Hell Mary.

Seba – a giant ghost and the most terrifying clown I've ever set eyes on – drops his head. "I'm sorry," he whispers.

I can't believe he's doing this for us. We had him all wrong.

"Prove it," she snaps, drawing herself up to her full height. "Get on your knees and beg me."

Seba grimaces, but he drops to his knees.

"Mary, I'm begging you to release them unharmed. You've got everything you wanted…"

"Almost… Give me your tether to seal the deal and I'll let the children go. Come on, out with it." She snaps her ring-clad fingers and holds out her left hand.

He wiggles his gold tooth loose with his tongue and spits it into her hand. Both Rusty and I flinch. It's utterly revolting, but she seems delighted.

"We can get it reset into a new ring. We can renew our vows!"

"What about the children?" grunts Seba.

"Oh, yes, yes, the children," says Hell Mary, like we're some minor irritation unworthy of her attention. "Amit. Amira. Put them on the boat with the ferryman. I'm sure they can make their way back to the station from there."

Now we've delivered what she wanted, we're of no use to her. She doesn't see us as a threat.

I look at the trapped performers. Despite all our grand plans, we've failed them. We've failed everyone.

"*Let them go and give us back our parents,*" I say.

Rusty looks ready to rush Hell Mary.

"*Spookmiths to the—*"

Amira grabs Rusty's arm and marches him out of the tent.

"Don't you get it?" says Amit, grabbing me and pulling me after him.

"Seba is buying you time," explains Amira. "Hell Mary will be so busy trying to recreate some great love story between her and Seba that you'll have a chance to search the fairground."

Rusty and I stop struggling. We allow Amit and Amira to lead us through a sea of smaller tents away from the big top and the Death Shadows.

My emotions calm the further we get from Hell Mary. I share a hug with Amira and because I'm disappearing she sort of sinks through my skin into my bones. It's all kinds of yuck so I don't hug her for too long.

"*Thank you,*" says Rusty.

"We'll tell Hell Mary we left you with the ferryman," says

Amit. "I wish we could help you find your parents, but she'll notice if we're gone too long and will come looking."

"Good luck," calls Amira, as they leave us.

We're going to need more than luck and I'm about to tell Rusty that, when a figure steps out of the darkness.

18

"What are you doing here?" I snap. Traitor Joe hovers uncertainly beside a lopsided tent.

"I want to help," he says. "I should have told you I'd made a deal with Hell Mary. I should have warned you I was leading you into a trap."

Joe's voice is too much for Troy. He launches himself from Rusty's pocket and into Joe's arms with a squeal of joy.

A flash of disbelief travels across Joe's face, followed by a loud sob.

"Troy!" he cries, hugging the little rat to

his chest, tears of happiness welling in his eyes. "You found him."

Troy snuggles into Joe's arms. It's pretty cute, and their obvious happiness at being reunited dissolves a lot of my anger. Joe isn't the only person to have got things wrong because of love. He was prepared to do anything to get Troy back, while Rusty and I brought the Show Stone to Hell Mary because we love our parents. It doesn't make it right, but it does go some way to explaining our actions.

A single howl goes up from a Death Shadow in the distance. We need to get moving.

"*We helped you out, now you need to help us,*" I say.

"I'll do anything you ask," says Joe. "You brought Troy back to me."

"*We need to find the mirror maze,*" I explain. "*Can you help?*"

Joe nods and Troy squeaks. "Let's go."

Another howl. Closer this time. We've got to hurry.

"*Let's split up,*" says Rusty. "*We can cover more ground that way.*"

Rusty and Fang go left. Joe and Troy go right. Which just leaves little old me with the straight-ahead option. I really wish Phrank was with me. He's a bad-tempered pheasant who is used to getting his own way, but we share a Spooksmith bond and right now I could really do with the company.

The fairground is dark and muddy and miserable. It couldn't be further from the sparkling and beautiful Starlight Circus that Mac talked about. I peer into dimly lit tents, and rickety sheds and stumble across a half-constructed, wooden amphitheatre. Hell Mary seems to keep changing her mind as to what she wants. Everything looks as though it's been abandoned halfway through.

"*Indigo.*"

I jump, covering my mouth to stifle a scream.

"Rusty, you can't sneak up—"

He's panting, out of breath from sprinting over to me. "*Joe's found the mirror maze!*"

My tiredness falls away.

"*It's Mum and Dad! Come on!*" he urges.

We run towards the river, darting between buildings and tents, keeping an eye out for any approaching Death Shadows. Thankfully, none of them appear to have picked up our trail. We're in Seba's debt for keeping Hell Mary distracted.

"Quick! In here!" says Joe, ushering us inside a tent, before leading us through an opening in the far wall.

It's not until I'm on the other side of the canvas that I realize we're not outside – the darkness is too thick and the quiet too heavy.

Joe strikes a match and lights a single candle.

I gasp as a hundred other candles flare all around us. It takes me a moment to realize they're just reflections.

We're in the mirror maze. We're only one step away from saving Mum and Dad. The maze isn't a prison, it's a place of light and hope.

Rusty can't contain himself. "*If you can hear us, we're coming!*" he shouts.

There's no noise from inside the maze, but there's a howl from outside.

"*Great work, Rusty. Now the Death Shadows know exactly where to find us,*" I snap.

I take the candle from Joe and push ahead, padding along wooden planks into what can only be a warehouse beside the river. A few steps in and the mirrored corridor branches out three ways.

Fang pokes his head out of Rusty's coat pocket and squeaks something.

"*Keep right,*" says Rusty.

"*Did Fang tell you that?*" I ask, only half-sarcastically.

Rusty rolls his eyes. "*Mazes have rules. Pick a direction and stick to it. If you pick right, stay right. If you pick left, stay left.*"

Somewhere, in the distance, I hear the faint boom of the city clock striking five. The mirrors shiver with the vibration.

"*But what if we hit a dead end?*" I say. "*Mum and Dad are running out of time!*"

"*This place is the stuff of nightmares,*" grumbles Rusty.

"*It's about to get worse,*" I say.

"*Don't say it,*" says Rusty.

"Say what?" says Joe.

"*We're going to have to split up again.*"

"*I knew you were going to say that,*" mutters Rusty.

"*I don't like it either, but we have no choice.*"

Joe hands out more candles and peels off first. Then it's Rusty's turn. I clasp my lit candle tightly, holding it out in front of me like a shield against the darkness.

I have to stop myself from running after Rusty. Silence presses down on me, reminding me of when I was lost in Greyscar Mine. I try to ignore it, scurrying down the left-hand route. The only thing worse than being lost and alone in a maze is being lost in one with Death Shadows and Hell Mary for company.

The candle gives off no warmth and my core is like an iceberg.

There's a draught and the candle flares. I catch a glimpse of something moving behind me, but when I stare directly into the mirror ahead, it shows nothing, not even my own reflection.

A cold sweat bubbles under my skin.

Why can't I see myself? I'm standing right here. Is it too late? Am I already a ghost?

I push the candle forwards until it and my fingertips hit the mirror. The surface of it ripples like waves on a pond and then it mists over.

My body goes rigid as writing starts to appear on the other side.

Hell Mary. Hell Mary. Hell Mary.

I mouth the words aloud before I realize what I'm doing, and a figure appears in the distance, somehow inside the mirror, as though it exists on another plane.

It's too dark to really see who the figure is, but the goosebumps all over my body know. A long black dress sweeps towards me, and a head covered with a lace veil lifts in my direction.

I've said her name three times in a mirror. Hell Mary is here to show my future. And unlike the reflection in the hotel mirror, this one has its sights set on me.

I need to look away, break the spell, but I can't... My eyes are fixed on the mirror and the predator on the other side.

Mirror Hell Mary lifts a ring-clad finger and scratches a word into the glass with a long, sharp nail:

DEATH

Is it my death or Mum and Dad's? Either way, that word is like a dagger. It shreds my hope, leaving me empty.

Hell Mary removes her veil to reveal a grinning skull. No flesh, no soft tissue, just stone-cold bone.

She reaches a grasping hand out of the mirror, towards my eyes. I scream and drop the candle.

19

In an instant, Rusty is beside me. He scoops a stone from the floor and throws it at the mirror, shattering the glass. Hell Mary disappears, but I can't get that grinning skull out of my brain, or that word: DEATH.

"Indigo!" Rusty shakes my shoulders. "*She's not really here. It's okay.*"

I blink like I'm waking from a nightmare. "*It's too late...*"

"*It won't be too late if you get a move on!*" says Rusty, pushing me forward. "*Joe's found Mum and Dad.*"

Those words, "Mum and Dad", cut through the despair quicker than any other. Despite everything, we might be able to save them. I sprint after Rusty, marvelling at how he's remembered the way, when I step on something small and hard. I look down to see a little plastic monster. It's one of Rusty's Battle Beast models. That must have been what he was collecting from the bags back at the station.

"I was in too much of a hurry to stay right and I didn't have any breadcrumbs like Hansel and Gretel," he explains. *"So, I improvised."*

Sometimes, I'm reminded that underneath his nasty taste in T-shirts, my brother is pretty smart. This is one of those times.

We weave through the maze until we find Joe at the centre. He's standing in a three-metre square space, surrounded by mirrors and flickering candles. He's guarding my parents. They are slumped on the ground, their skin becoming increasingly see-through by the second.

It's like looking at bodies with the life draining out of them. I run to Mum and Dad, and search for a pulse.

"It's faint, but they're still with us," I say, lowering my head with relief. *"But we need to get them out of here. Fast."*

Rusty puts Dad over his shoulder with ease and I drop my candle and pick up Mum. She's so light it's like carrying an empty bottle. Even if we get them home, will they recover?

Joe goes ahead, holding a candle to light our way, following Rusty's Battle Beast trail.

We've just started back when a Death Shadow howls. It's impossible to tell where the sound came from when it echoes all around us. I shift what little there is of Mum's weight to the other shoulder.

"*Please tell me there's another way out,*" I say.

"*There's only one way out of a maze,*" says Rusty. "*That's the whole point.*"

I'm in the middle of our little group, Mum on my left shoulder while reaching out with my right hand into the darkness. I'm feeling my way around a mirror when my index finger brushes something etched into the glass.

"*Joe,*" I whisper, "*bring me the light.*"

Joe holds the candle up to the mirror. It illuminates a riddle: *Looking for freedom? Waltz three times to find a ring that's part of the furniture.*

"*I thought mazes weren't supposed to have cheat notes,*" I say.

"Maybe the workers Hell Mary got to build her maze didn't like her very much. What better way to undermine her than to ruin her maze?" asks Joe.

"*Anyone know how to waltz?*" I ask.

Without discussing it, Rusty shifts Dad from over his shoulder to out in front of him, Dad's feet on top of his. Then he begins to dance, one step forward, one to the right, then feet together. He rotates as he dances an unconscious Dad down the line of mirrors, making three one-quarter turns before he stops. Wedged into a gap down the side of the mirror in front of him is a metal ring about the size of a large doughnut.

I lean forward and take the ring out of the gap. It has a small, notched hole in the front.

"*Remind me to stop teasing you about watching* Dance Your Feet Off *reruns,*" I say.

Rusty grins.

I turn the metal ring over.

"*Roll me to find the thing you can answer but will never talk back,*" I read. "*I've no idea what that means, but here goes...*"

I roll the ring along the floor. The ring goes forward in a straight line to begin with but then several mirrors ahead, it veers sharply off to the right.

"The floor slopes away here," says Joe.

"*And there's a breeze,*" says Rusty.

"*The thing you can answer but never talks back is a door!*" I say excitedly.

If it is a door, there must be some sort of lever or handle in the mirror. All I find is a thin piece of metal. I put Mum down and pull and twist and turn the metal spindle. Nothing happens. Another howl echoes through the maze from the Death Shadows. I start tugging on the spindle with more urgency, but my sweaty palms just slip right off it.

"*My turn,*" says Rusty.

He puts Dad down and picks up the ring from the floor. He lines up the hole in the ring with the metal spindle and then pushes it on. The *click* as it locks into place almost makes me want to hug him. He turns the ring, and the mirror swings open onto a loading dock above the Other Thames.

We grab our parents and leap outside, sucking in the air and embracing the freedom.

The dock is suspended on stilts above water. I can see it rushing by through the gaps in the boards under my feet. Once the others are next to me, I put Mum down and slam the mirror shut.

"*There's no way to lock it from this side,*" I say as another howl goes up from the Death Shadow inside the warehouse.

"*And there's no way off this wharf that doesn't involve swimming,*" says Rusty.

I say some words that my parents probably wouldn't be proud that I know and then I spot a hunched figure on the muddy beach upstream.

"*It's the ferryman,*" I say.

Rusty puts Dad down and runs to the end of the wharf.

"*Basil!*" yells Rusty. "*Basil! Over here!*"

Basil stares in every direction until he finally looks towards the loading dock.

"You owe me an artefact!" he yells.

"*Well, come over here and get it!*" I yell back.

Rusty empties his pockets as Basil drags his boat into the water and rows towards us. My brother is holding two Battle Beast figurines, my stuffed toy tiger from the zoo and a chicken leg.

Fang pokes his head out of Rusty's pocket and squeaks angrily.

"*Yeah, I know it's yours, but I need you to give it up.*"

Fang squeaks something that sounds very like the word "no".

"*I'll buy you a whole packet of chicken legs when we get home,*" says Rusty.

Fang gives a squeak of acceptance and disappears back inside Rusty's coat.

"*Phrank would never be that difficult,*" I say.

"*We both know Phrank would have demanded a year's supply of sunflower seeds!*"

"*What can I say? He knows his own mind.*"

Basil pulls alongside the wharf as a Death Shadow starts to slide beneath the door of the warehouse, bringing with it a drop in temperature and an air of doom.

"Look out!" cries Joe.

We all scramble down the rickety wooden ladder towards the boat, Rusty and me with our parents slung across our shoulders.

The boat wobbles as we clamber aboard and Basil steadies it, but he makes no move to row us away.

"Artefacts," booms Basil's voice from beneath his hood.

Rusty chucks everything he has onto the floor of the boat. The items land with a clatter.

"Interesting," says Basil, admiring one of the models. "I would like to know its provenance. Where did—"

"*Just get us out of here!*" I yell as a cloud of cold air envelopes the boat.

At the top of the wharf a Death Shadow is peering down at us with murderous intent.

Basil finally picks up his oars and steers us out into the middle of the river.

"*That was close*," says Rusty, holding his chest.

"*Way too close*," I agree, and then I grin. "*But we did it. We got Mum and Dad, and we've got time to spare.*"

"Back to that model," says Basil, dropping his oars now

he's got us away from the Death Shadows. "How old is it?"

"*I bought it and painted it at Battle Beast Universe yesterday afternoon*," says Rusty. I've never heard him annoyed when talking about Battle Beast before. "*I'll tell you all about it, but please, can you just take us downriver?*"

A shout goes up from the riverbank.

"Over there," says Joe.

It's Amit and Amira with Mac and Hercules Helen. They're standing beneath an old dock light, waving madly.

I wave back. It's time for phase two of the plan.

Rusty unhooks the whistle from around his neck. He hands it to Joe, who is busy cuddling Troy.

"What's this for?"

"*We need you to get Mum and Dad on that train before the clock strikes six*," says Rusty.

The original plan was for Rusty and me to take our parents to the train and then double back to find the Show Stone and help the performers. I shuffle uncomfortably on the hard, wooden bench. Getting Joe to help will certainly speed things up, but can we rely on him?

"*We're trusting you with the most important people in our lives,*" I say.

"For the people who brought Troy back to me, I'll do anything. You can trust me."

"*Blow the whistle to summon the train and watch out for the ticket inspector,*" says Rusty.

"What about you two?" asks Joe.

"*We've got a Show Stone to steal,*" I say.

20

Basil drops Joe and my parents on the far bank of the river before rowing Rusty and me back across it.

"I get to keep *all* the artefacts if I wait and take you on one final crossing?" asks Basil, as he spots Fang nibbling on the chicken leg.

"*Yes, everything,*" I say, placing a very annoyed-looking Fang in Rusty's arms minus the chicken leg.

"*Can we just talk about that last Battle Beast miniature for a second?*" asks Rusty.

"That's my favourite," says Basil. "I like

the bright colours and the jam dripping down its front."

"*That's supposed to be blood,*" says Rusty, sounding a bit put out.

I stifle a snigger.

The performers are waiting for us as we disembark.

"You ready for this?" asks Mac.

"*Of course we are,*" I say. "*We're Spooksmiths.*"

"*Where's the Show Stone?*" asks Rusty.

"I'm pretty sure she took it to her private tent," says Amit.

"*Then that's where we're going,*" I say.

We weave our way back through the fairground, keeping low, using the tents and buildings around us to hide. The Death Shadows haven't picked up our scent again and are still hunting for us over at the warehouse.

"Here," says Amira, stopping outside a blood-red tent.

There are raised voices inside. They belong to Hell Mary and Seba.

"Let's not waste time blaming one another," says Hell Mary.

"You've got nothing to blame me for," says Seba.

"Really?"

"Really."

"What about that little trick you pulled with the ring? And you convinced me that the Show Stone and my star performers were already in Necropolis City."

Seba stays quiet. There's no arguing with the truth.

"I know everything and I'm willing to forgive you. I may even find a way to let you keep that disgusting and forbidden dog."

Bunnykins yaps his disapproval.

"Why?"

"What if I said that I missed you," says Hell Mary.

Seba hoots with laughter and leaves the tent.

"Playing hard to get? How sweet," Hell Mary yells after him. "I'll play along but don't forget that I own you!"

There's a snap of the canvas as Hell Mary goes after him.

"*Dead romantic,*" whispers Rusty. "*Get it? They're dead and Hell Mary's trying to be—*"

I groan. "*I get it. But now's our chance.*"

We slip inside. The interior is even more unfriendly than I'd imagined. It reminds me of a tomb. Black gauze hangs from the ceiling like spider's webs and candles and incense litter the floor. It smells of smoke and tobacco and death, creating a heavy, soupy scent that makes me gag and Rusty hold his nose.

Something glimmers towards the back of the tent, through the gauze and smoke. I pause. It's the Show Stone, shot through with the deep red of the circus performers' blood.

The metal cage around it has been removed and it's sitting on a table cradled between two glass hands.

Just looking at it fills me with disgust. The Stone is Hell Mary's most prized possession, her way of controlling her performers and the reason she took my parents. And yet, she's nowhere to be seen...

A spark of genuine satisfaction runs through me at the thought that I'm about to make her arrogance her downfall. She assumed that with Rusty and I gone, and the performers bullied into submission, no one would dare touch it.

Well, she didn't count on me. This is my chance to put things right. I snatch it from the cradle.

From the moment my hands touch the glass, cold like I've never felt before shoots through my veins. When I took the Stone from the hotel, it was wrapped in a metal cage and my coat. Now there's nothing between it and me. It's like holding onto winter.

My hands stick to its surface, great icy waves flowing up my arms to frostbite my brain.

"*Indigo, are you okay?*" I can hear Rusty's voice, but it's muffled, like I'm underwater.

I'm drained, but the ball glows brighter with a freezing, blue light, as though it's feeding off my energy. The blood inside the ball swirls, turning it opaque before floating to the outer edges like oil separating in water. I remember what Hell Mary said about the Stone showing your past and your future. Then the images start to appear. Blurry shapes quickly form into figures and then faces. Faces I know...

I gasp. There's Mum and Dad and Grandpa... They're ageing backwards like I'm watching their lives rewinding.

"*Nana,*" I whisper.

Rusty and I never met Grandpa's wife, but we've both seen photographs. Warm and fuzzy love floods my brain as I realize the chubby little baby balanced on Nana's lap is Dad. He looks so sweet and happy without a care in the world. I just want him back.

I clasp the ball harder and the images start to flash faster. It's like being trapped in a speeding car with a reckless driver. I don't know what I'm doing or how to control what I'm seeing, but the Stone seems to have a destination in mind. My mouth is dry, my hands clenched. All I can do is hold on and go along for the ride.

The images slow and three figures appear in the mist: a teenage boy and two teenage girls in old-fashioned, Victorian clothing. They're on a beach, their feet leaving a trail of footprints in the sand. The curve of the bay reminds me of somewhere...then I spot the cliff-top churchyard and my stomach lurches.

I don't want to recognize it. I don't want any part of all this weirdness to be familiar, but there's no escaping the fact that I'm looking at something that happened in my hometown: Greyscar.

It's sunset in the vision and there's a small fire on the beach. One of the girls is holding a candle and the other one is drawing a triangle in the sand. I hold my breath as she adds the letters V.S., M.I. and L.W. to the three corners.

They're the same initials as on the crypt wall at home and on the whistle… Why am I getting the feeling that I should know them? Who are these people? My brain is racing to process what I'm seeing and my hands are shaking from the shock and the cold. Part of me wants to shut my eyes, but I can't tear them away.

The vision zooms in on the teenagers, pulling in and out again like a photographer with a problematic lens. Finally, it focuses on a single face.

It's one of the girls. She has messy dark curls, gappy teeth and a very familiar nose with a slight downward slope…just like mine. It's obvious she's a Smith. The V.S. initials must belong to her. I peer closer. I'm pretty sure she's in one of the portraits on the ancestor wall at home. My jaw tenses. I wish I'd paid more attention to those gloomy old paintings. They all have names underneath, but I've no idea what the V stands for.

As though the crystal ball knows I'm not going to get anything more from this particular face, it refocuses on the other girl. She's blond and slight. I don't recognize her at all. The focus shifts again, this time onto the boy. I blink rapidly, my brain struggling to compute what my eyes are showing me. He's not the way I remember him. He's younger and there's no moustache or ghostly flies, but the big bushy eyebrows and small, darting eyes are unmistakably his. It's the original, human (and alive) version of Malachi Innspectre.

The atmosphere is heavy and brooding and my head aches from this overload of spooky information. I've got a feeling this is just the beginning and that everything I've seen so far is leading up to something big.

The three teenagers move to separate corners of the triangle. I tense as my Smith ancestor lights the candle. It's black and twisted like a rope and it smokes horribly. Dread drifts into the room as though carried here by the smoke in the vision. I want to yell at the girl to stop and put the candle out, but I find my voice is as frozen as my hands.

There's rustling to my left, but I keep my eyes locked on the crystal ball. If I look away now, I'll miss the most important part of this vision. It's all been building towards whatever I'm about to see next. I can feel it in my bones.

The teenagers on the beach are chanting. A black hole has

opened in the centre of the fire and an absence of light is reaching out with long clawed hands. Death Shadow hands...

"*Rusty to the rescue!*" comes a cry.

There's a flurry of activity beside me and I blink. The vision blurs and disappears as a black tablecloth is thrown over the ball.

"*No!*" I yell.

"*Indigo, snap out of it!*" Rusty's yelling at me but it takes me a moment to fully register where I am and what's happening. "*Hell Mary's—*"

"Here," she announces, cackling. "And it would seem that you have something that belongs to me."

21

Hell Mary's laughter echoes around the tent.

"I knew you were coming back for it," Hell Mary says. "My Show Stone never lies. What did it reveal to you, Indigo Spooksmith?"

Rusty gives me a *What's she on about?* look. The vision must only be visible to the person holding the Stone.

I shake my head. *Not now.*

"Did it show you that your powers are stolen and unnatural?"

I'm not sure what I saw, but it looked like

a Death Shadow reaching out of the fire towards my ancestor. What I do know is that I want to see more. It's like there's an invisible string attaching me to the Stone now and it's pulling at me to see the end of that vision.

"*There's nothing 'natural' about you or your powers,*" says Rusty.

"Well said!" says Seba, entering the tent. "I hope I haven't missed all the fun."

The rest of the performers file in behind him. Hell Mary raises an eyebrow.

"I see we have an audience." Hell Mary smiles. "Come, give me back my Stone and I will help you to make sense of what you have seen. Allow your past to inform your future. I can be your guide."

The Stone's secrets are crying out to be revealed, tugging me in a direction I don't want to go but I'm finding hard to resist.

"Don't listen to her," says Mac.

Hell Mary glares at Mac and he shrinks back. She shakes her head, her necklaces tinkling as she moves. "If Indigo doesn't listen to me, she will remain in the dark. Go on, remove the cloth..."

Can it really hurt? Maybe just one more glimpse... I remove the cloth from the Show Stone.

"I think you are starting to understand," says Hell Mary. "It's irresistible. I knew you would feel the same as me. Desire for the Stone is something one cannot fight."

My hands are tingling with the Stone's cold power. All that history – my family's history – floats just beneath a brittle layer of glass.

"*Indigo,*" says Rusty. "*Look at me.*"

"Don't listen to him," says Hell Mary, dismissing him with a tinkle of her ring-clad fingers.

"*Indigo, Hell Mary's not helping you. It'll be another trick. She only thinks about herself,*" pleads Rusty.

I hear him but I don't want to look away. A deep hunger for the truths only the Stone can reveal is building inside of me. The only way to fill that hunger is to stare into it and let it show me its secrets.

The blood within the Stone starts to swirl.

"*You look into that Stone and Hell Mary wins,*" says Rusty.

Rusty's words finally sink in. She's playing me, but it's like my eyeballs are stuck to the glass. Peeling them away from the Stone physically hurts. With a super Spooksmith effort, I force myself to meet my brother's gaze.

"*Now, look at them.*" He gestures to the performers.

They are huddled behind Hell Mary like frightened mice. Blade is cuddling Mac, Amit and Amira are holding hands, the clown troupe and the jugglers are huddled together wide-eyed, while Hercules Helen, Ray and the contortionist are frozen in various poses of disbelief. Even Seba is waiting for me to snap out of it.

I blink. What am I doing? Hell Mary has to be stopped. She can't be allowed to control these poor people any longer.

Whatever hold the Stone had over me is gone. It's clear now that there's only one course of action that will free the performers trapped in the Stone for good.

I raise the Show Stone above my head, looking at the performers for agreement before I make my next move.

They all nod their heads.

"You wouldn't..." warns Hell Mary.

"*Watch me.*" And using all my energy, I bring my arms down fast, releasing the Stone at shoulder height and sending it plummeting onto the hard wooden planks.

I shield my face, expecting it to shatter into a million pieces on impact. But when I turn back, the only visible damage is a hairline crack in the blood-red quartz.

Mouth dry, I start to shiver. I've messed up yet again.

Hell Mary screams with laughter. It reminds me of a hyena right before it rips into a kill.

The Show Stone rolls towards her, and she lifts it up to inspect it.

"You will have to do better than that, you little—" She starts to gloat, but stops abruptly. Her next word is a whispered: "No."

That one little word is all I need to stop shivering. I look up to see a crack in the Stone. A crack that is growing, splintering off in all directions like roads on a map.

Hell Mary screams again, but this time it's a scream of despair. She tenderly cups her hands around the Stone like it's the face of someone she loves, and that person is slipping away. It does no good. The Stone's injuries are terminal, and the cracks keep spreading.

"What have you done?" she moans.

I don't answer and neither does anyone else. We are all too busy watching the show.

Separate sections of the glass are bulging outwards as though some force is pushing them from the other side. Hell Mary is forcing them back down like she's playing Whack-a-Mole, her rings clinking against the stone.

But she's fighting a losing battle.

There's a *wumpf* from inside the Stone followed by a *boom* so loud I cover my ears. The Stone explodes. Pieces of glass scatter across the floor like spilled ice cubes and the performers' blood fades from red to pink to white and then evaporates.

"We're free!" says Mac, twirling Blade around.

The clowns dance a little jig and Hercules Helen joins in.

"NO!" howls Hell Mary.

But she can't do anything to them. Her power over them is gone.

"Thank you!" shouts Mac as he starts to disappear.

"Goodbye," shout the clowns.

Blade gives a little salute with one of her knives and Hercules Helen waves. Then they blink out of existence. In this realm at least.

"You children will pay for this! I will scratch out your eyes! Remove your spleens! Eat your livers!"

"I think we've made her angry," whispers Rusty.

"I'm not done yet," I say, folding my arms.

"That's what I hoped you'd say," says Rusty.

I leap aside as Hell Mary lunges towards me with clawed hands. But I've got my eye on something else: the jet pendant with the mirrored surface around her neck. I noticed the way she caressed it when she talked about tethers the first time we met her.

It catches the candlelight, and Hell Mary's unveiled reflection winks at me from the mirror like it knows a secret. I'm pretty sure I'm staring at the answer to all our problems.

The mirrored necklace is somehow holding her reflection

from before she became a veil-wearing skeleton. It's her tether, the thing that's allowed her image to appear in mirrors.

Rusty's also staring at the necklace, like he's put the pieces together too.

We both dive for it, but Hell Mary's fast. She grasps our outstretched hands, snatching them down and away from her with such force that it jars my shoulder.

"So, you've worked it out," she says with a sneer. "My tether is my reflection. Once I learned that, I was able to send it anywhere. All it took was for someone to stare back at me and they dropped down dead!"

I can see Fang creeping higher up inside Rusty's pocket, ready to launch himself at her. All I need to do is distract her by keeping her talking.

"*People dropped down dead because you scratched out their eyes?*" I ask.

"That was just a phase." Hell Mary laughs. "I discovered heart attacks were much quicker and less messy."

"*Murderer,*" I say.

Hell Mary focuses all her gloating on me...just as Fang flies out of Rusty's pocket and launches himself at her neck. She screams, releasing our wrists so she can fight him off, clawing and scratching like a wild cat. He clings on, managing to chew through the black silk holding the mirrored pendant before Hell Mary shakes herself, flinging both Fang and the necklace from her body.

Rusty catches Fang, but the necklace slips through my fingers.

Then Seba steps out of the shadows. If it's possible, Seba looks even more menacing than Hell Mary. His painted face has cracked to look like a mosaic and his red smile has bled down his chin. He snatches the necklace from the air.

"Seba..." says Hell Mary. There's a warning note to her voice, as though she's daring him to defy her.

A mixture of emotions from sadness to childlike happiness flicker across his clown face, as though he's remembering the life they'd shared. Eventually though, his face settles into a picture of resignation and his mouth into a thin line of blood-red determination.

"Goodbye, Mary," he croaks and throws the necklace to me.

I don't hesitate. I catch it and drop it to the floor, crushing Hell Mary's tether under my heel. There's a sharp crack as the mirrored necklace splinters. Dust pours out from the necklace and everything that makes Hell Mary, Hell Mary – her lace dress and veil, her necklace and her rings – starts falling off her like a snake shedding its skin.

"You cannot defeat me!" she yells.

And then she looks at her hands and starts to scream. Her bony white fingers are crumbling. She rocks forward as her left foot collapses and then both her legs give way. Followed by her arms.

"*Grim,*" says Rusty.

It is, but neither of us can look away.

She's like a tree with its roots and branches cut off. It's all kinds of wrong. Next, her body collapses and her neck, until all that's left is her snapping skull.

She works her lower jaw, jumping towards us like a devil bunny.

"Curse you!" she cries, her teeth clacking together. "Spooksmiths will meet a bitter end!"

The bottom part of her jaw breaks down, silencing her for good. Just like with the circus performers, destroying Hell Mary's tether means she's been pulled into whatever afterlife comes next. Everyone is staring, transfixed, as her skull disintegrates, leaving Hell Mary as nothing more than a pile of bone-white ash.

22

I'm so happy that we've defeated Hell Mary, I could almost hug Rusty. Almost.

We settle for a high five.

Bunnykins leaps out of Seba's arms. He digs through Hell Mary's ashy remains until he locates Seba's gold tooth. He drops it into Seba's hand and Seba puts the tooth back in his mouth just as the first chimes of six o'clock ring out across the fairground.

It's an eerie sound, like the tolling of a church bell at a funeral, and I wrap my arms around myself.

"*I hope Joe got Mum and Dad on the train home,*" says Rusty.

"*Me too,*" I say. "*How about we join them?*"

Hell Mary made it very clear that Mum and Dad needed to be out of Necropolis City by the stroke of six. She said Rusty and I had longer because of our powers, but she wasn't exactly the trustworthy type.

Amira picks up her own tooth tether from Hell Mary's remains and the rest of the performers follow her lead.

"*Will you be okay now Hell Mary's gone?*" I ask.

"We'll be able to rebuild the circus the way we want to," says Amira.

"Or move on," says Amit.

And I know they'll be okay now, because they're in charge of their own endings.

"If you want to go home, we'd better leave before the Death Shadows get here," says Seba.

"We'll hold them off," says Ray.

We exchange quick hugs and goodbyes with the other performers. We've been through so much together, I wish we had longer.

Amira pulls me towards her and we hug like old friends.

"Maybe we'll meet again one day," she says.

"*If we do, I'd like a bit less kidnapping and mortal danger,*" I say.

Seba coughs and taps his giant clown shoes. "Come on," he says. "You're not out of mortal danger yet. Follow me and stick close."

Fang burrows deeper into Rusty's pocket and we're off, out of the tent and running so fast my legs are at the limit of my control.

Dawn is breaking, a grey, bleak light drained of all colour. Unless they've made that train, I'm very aware that it's my parents' death sentence written in the sky.

We charge across the fairground. I've no idea how Ray and the other performers are going to help us get away – everywhere I look, more Shadows are appearing, forming a defensive line around the perimeter. There's a *whoosh* followed by a *crackle* and suddenly the fairground is bathed in orange light.

"*Ray is torching the tents!*" says Rusty.

The Death Shadows stop their advance. First one, then another, and another Death Shadow moves towards the burning tents.

"*They're drawn to the light,*" I whisper.

We reach the river and climb aboard Basil's waiting boat as the fairground burns.

Only six weeks ago, Rusty and I were running from the Cinderman and a whole town-load of zombies. Now we're racing across a dead city with a giant clown to catch a ghost train while trying to escape a squadron of Death Shadows.

"*You can't call life as a Spooksmith boring,*" says Rusty.

Basil, our cloaked and hooded ferryman, has Rusty's Battle Beast figurines tied around his neck on an old bit of string. The chicken leg is in pride of place, tied to the bow of his boat. Fang is watching it and salivating.

We climb out of the boat on the other side and wave Basil goodbye. I have to help Seba, because he's got one of his giant shoes stuck underneath one of the seats. By the time we reach the square, the doll death clock reads 6:20.

Troy spots us first as we enter the station and starts up a cacophony of squeaks, which Fang answers.

Joe waves. He's waiting on the platform.

"I put them on the train and sent them back like you said."

"*Thank you,*" I say, and I don't think I've ever meant something so deeply.

But "thank you" isn't enough for Rusty. He throws his arms around Joe. "*Friends for life,*" he says.

"And death," Joe says.

He returns the whistle, and Rusty uses it to summon the train.

Somewhere out in the void between worlds, there's an answering call.

"*I guess this is it,*" I say, and turn to Seba. "*Goodbye and—*"

"Bunnykins and I are coming with you," says Seba. "Someone needs to make sure all those animals in the pet cemetery are reunited with their owners."

I grin. "*That's a great idea. I'll make sure Malachi understands.*"

And Seba gives me something that might be a genuine smile, although all the smudged make-up makes it look creepy as hell.

"Oh no you don't!" The officious ticket collector is storming towards us. "You two look half-dead. You are staying right here, and that clown is going nowhere either!"

It's true, we're not looking our best. I can see all the way through Rusty to the buildings on the other side of the station. He's like one of those South American glass frogs with their transparent skin, except I can't see his organs, which I'm thankful for. I really don't want to be faced with Rusty's guts.

The chug of the train is getting closer, but so is something else. If I didn't know better, I'd ignore it, but unfortunately that's not an option.

Howls erupt like the cries of hungry wolves.

My eyes meet Rusty's.

"*Death Shadows,*" he says.

We're so close to freedom I could scream, but we're trapped until the train comes, and the ticket collector isn't helping...

"They're over here!" he yells towards the Death Shadows. "Come and get them!"

Seba growls and launches himself at the ticket collector, who squeals and scurries away back to his office.

Unfortunately, our other problems are not so easy to scare.

"Get as far down the platform as you can. We'll try to distract them," says Seba.

And he and Joe stand their ground, Bunnykins and Troy right beside them.

The howling increases and black shapes drift through the archway from the ticket office and onto the platform. There's an emptiness about the Death Shadows, a hopeless sort of finality, as though they really are the end, and nothing exists beyond them.

Fang squeaks and burrows deeper into Rusty's pocket and we run down the platform until we reach the end.

The *huff-puff* of the train's engine and the rumble of its wheels tells me the train is coming but the Death Shadows are closing in. There are six of them and they fan out, a blurry nightmare of nothingness.

The Death Shadows howl between themselves as though they're talking about who should kill who.

Seba and Joe have found candles and they're waving them around, trying to distract the Shadows with the light. For a single moment, I think it's going to work. The Death Shadows stop and circle Joe and Seba and the flames, while Bunnykins and Troy yap and squeak.

It's going to be close. The platform is only about six carriages long. If the train doesn't arrive soon, we've got nowhere left to run.

There's a screech of brakes and suddenly everything is covered by a thick grey fog of smoke and steam as the train pulls into the station. In my eagerness to get on board, I forget to prepare for the blast of the train's arrival. The shock wave unbalances me, and I pitch backwards.

A howl sounds right beside my ear, and something touches my arm.

It's icy and it sizzles like I've been branded. I scream as the pain and the cold spreads through my body like frost across a lake. The rush of blood in my veins is slowing.

The last thing I see is Rusty, and the look he gives me – like I'm leaving him – is one that will stay with me for ever. I fall backwards into the Death Shadow behind me. It acts like a hole in the floor, and I collapse inside it, arms flailing, vision narrowing. It's like I'm Alice tumbling down the rabbit hole. Rusty is getting further away. There's darkness all around me and nothing to stop my fall...

A warm hand suddenly grasps mine, jerking me back. My heart is speeding, my head spinning as I rush towards a pinprick of light that's getting bigger and bigger by the second.

With a blinding flash, the darkness disappears and I'm back, standing on the platform, my hand clasped in Rusty's. Determination is fixed on his face. I've never seen him look this way, not even when he made the North-east Battle Beast final.

"*Don't leave me,*" he whispers, his voice breaking.

I shake my head, tears filling my eyes. "*Never,*" I whisper.

Our brother–sister bonding moment is broken by a loud howl. The smoke has cleared and in front of us is a Death Shadow. A candle is on the floor between us. Rusty must have thrown it to distract the Death Shadow and save me. The flame has gone out and I can sense that this shadow of death is now boiling mad. It pulls itself up to its full height, looming over us like a storm cloud. Sensing an easy kill, the other Death Shadows close in.

"*If this is goodbye—*" starts Rusty.

"*—then we go together,*" I finish, gripping his hand tighter.

"Not if I can help it," says Joe, running to our side.

"Or me," says Seba, slapping his giant shoes on the floor as though daring the Shadows to approach for a kicking.

"That won't be necessary," says a voice I recognize.

The door at the front of the train swings open and out steps Malachi Innspectre. His face is fierce and buzzing with angry flies, his knee-length coat billowing with them. He leaps from the train to stand between us and the Death Shadows. A ghost made of flies defending us against shadowy grim reapers. It's pretty out-there, but then again, we're Spooksmiths and out-there is our new normal.

"Leave them!" shouts Malachi, addressing the Death Shadows.

They howl at him, obviously furious, but they don't come any closer. In this moment, Malachi is just as scary as they are.

He turns to Rusty and me.

"Your parents have arrived home safely. They are recovering in the Necropolis Railway chapel. Get on the train," he commands.

I've never ever felt such relief coupled with such utter exhaustion. We fall into the ghost train and collapse on the seats. Seba too.

"*We made it,*" I whisper.

"*We made it,*" Rusty repeats, clasping my hand.

The Death Shadows drift away, losing focus now they've been denied their prey.

We wave to Joe and Troy as the train pulls out of the station. I was too quick to judge Joe and now I'm sad I'll probably never see him or Troy again. But they've got each other, friends in life and death, and I hold onto that, warming my soul with the power of friendship, until the death stares opposite chill the mood.

Malachi is glaring at Seba and Seba is glaring back at him. I don't know if it's relief or tiredness or just the mind-blowing nature of our situation, but I find myself laughing. Rusty joins in and the train dives into the darkness, spiriting us away.

23

"That was the most reckless, dangerous and foolhardy thing I have ever seen!" says Malachi, flies streaming off him as he rants. "Live humans travelling to the dead side! I told you I'd handle the Hell Mary investigation! What were you thinking?"

I roll over on the seat, so I'm staring up at him.

"We were thinking we needed to save our parents."

Malachi explodes. He literally has, like, the biggest ghost tantrum I've ever seen.

Bluebottles are ricocheting off the windows of the train and the buzzing has reached deafening levels. And then as suddenly as he started, he stops, mid-sentence.

"Show me your arm," he says.

Every single part of me is hurting. I'm freezing and burning up at the same time. I look down at my forearm, the one with the birthmark. It's the same as Rusty's – grey-blue and shaped like a fingerprint – except mine is now rippling like a grassy meadow in the wind.

I shudder, sitting up and rubbing at it.

"Indigo?" asks Rusty. *"What is it?"*

I hold my arm out towards him.

Rusty pulls up his own sleeve and screams. His birthmark is behaving in exactly the same way as mine. It's like tiny threadworms are burrowing under the skin.

"What the...?" Rusty looks up at Malachi and so does Fang.

Malachi's face has gone from furious to shocked in an instant. He pulls up his own sleeve.

The flies stop buzzing long enough for a smudge to appear on his arm and then it settles into a birthmark. It's an exact copy of ours. I'm lost for words.

"You need to tell me who you both are," says Malachi. "Start at the beginning and leave nothing out."

"I think I'll take this opportunity to have a little nap,"

says Seba, and he moves further down the carriage.

Rusty and I take it in turns to fill Malachi in on our Spooksmith past, or what little we know of it.

"Spooksmiths," says Malachi. He shakes his head, sinking back onto one of the seats as the train rumbles through the darkness. "I should have known."

"*Why should you know?*" I ask.

"*Why do we have the same birthmark?*" asks Rusty.

"I swore never to speak of it," says Malachi, putting his head in his hands.

I'm no longer tired or lost for words. And I'm not taking no for an answer. I stand up.

"*Your whistle was engraved with the letters V.S., M.I., L.W.*," I say. "*It's the same engraving that's on the wall of the crypt beneath our family's funeral parlour. The M.I. is you, isn't it?*"

Malachi nods miserably.

"*And the V.S... The S stands for Smith or Spooksmith, right?*"

"Spooksmith," he says.

There's a story here, an explanation as to why Rusty and I are the way we are. It's time to come clean about the vision.

"*I saw something in Hell Mary's Show Stone.*"

"*I knew something was going on when you held it. Your eyes were like...*" Rusty goes cross-eyed and pulls an ugly face.

Even after everything we've been through, my skin prickles with irritation. I ignore him and carry on.

"*It showed me Greyscar beach. There was a fire and a candle and three people.*" I pause, letting my words sink in. "*The boy looked like you...*"

Malachi turns pale, even for a ghost. "We made a mistake, a horrible mistake. I'm sorry, but I've vowed never to speak of it. It's best if you forget what you saw—"

"*I can't. Ghosts keep coming after me and my family. First the Cinderman. Now Hell Mary. We need to arm ourselves with the truth.*"

"I personally assure you that what happened with Hell Mary will never happen again."

"*Too right it won't,*" says Rusty. "*We turned her to dust.*"

"*We're Spooksmiths. We deal with ghostly problems our way,*" I say, backing him up. "*But we could really do with a little background information. It turns out our ancestors didn't believe in writing things down.*"

"If I tell you more, it will only make things worse."

"*How will it make things worse than they already are?*"

"*We need answers,*" says Rusty, crossing his arms.

"The past should stay in the past. It's safer that way," says Malachi.

"*Rubbish,*" I say.

"*We can't know where we're going unless we know where we've been,*" adds Rusty.

I raise both eyebrows, impressed by his unexpectedly deep and thoughtful answer.

"*Battle Beast lore 321,*" he explains.

I roll my eyes and push ahead with the questioning. Malachi doesn't get to keep secrets when it threatens our family's safety.

"Who is L.W.? Is she the blond girl in the Show Stone vision?"

Malachi opens his mouth to speak, but his answer is drowned out by a screech of brakes. The train slows, sending me and Rusty sliding off the seats. Daylight spills into the carriage, a golden light like poured honey. My mood soars and I momentarily forget about the inquisition. I run to the window, followed by Rusty. We push our faces up against the glass, desperate for the heat of the sun after so long in the dark and the cold.

Dawn is breaking. I don't think I've ever seen anything so beautiful. Yellows and oranges blur together all the way up to a bright wintery blue sky. We're back on the other side, the living side, London proper.

As the train pulls into the Necropolis Railway Station, the rippling of our birthmarks stops. Rusty and I become more solid, while Malachi becomes more see-through.

There are still so many things we need answers to, but the most important question right now is: have Mum and Dad survived?

The train has barely come to a stop before Rusty and I are out and running to the chapel of rest, Fang running alongside.

Malachi has laid our parents out on the velvet-covered altar. They look a bit like human sacrifices up there, but they're more solid and there's colour in their cheeks, which is an improvement on the last time we saw them.

I hug Mum and when she stirs and hugs me back, I blink back tears of happiness.

"We can't let anything like this happen to them ever again," I say.

"Agreed," says Rusty, clinging tightly to Dad.

Malachi and Seba join us. Malachi is looking rather pained.

"*I've told him I'm commandeering his train for pet transportation,*" says Seba.

Bunnykins yips his approval.

"*I did not think it was appropriate to give animals an afterlife.*" Malachi sniffs. "*It was not what I was taught to believe.*"

"Animals have souls," I say. "It's not fair to keep them apart from their human companions."

"*I see that now,*" says Malachi.

"It's good to admit when you're wrong, but then you also need to be prepared to try and put things right," says Rusty.

"*I have agreed to accompany Seba to the pet cemetery and to try to reunite the dead in Necropolis City with their pets,*" says Malachi.

The memory of all those sad-eyed animals in the graveyard would have haunted me. "That's brilliant," I say. "Thank you for agreeing to do this."

"*He took a bit of persuading,*" mutters Seba.

"And thank you for helping us, Seba," says Rusty.

Now it's Seba's turn to look uncomfortable.

"*I'll try and scare some kids on the way back to the graveyard. Got to balance out all my good deeds,*" he says with a grin.

Mum is sitting up and blinking. "Who are you talking to?"

Seba cackles. "*Good luck!*"

Seba, Bunnykins and Malachi make their escape, leaving us to explain the unexplainable.

"What are we going to say?" I whisper.

"You're the oldest." Rusty smirks. "I'm going to leave it up to you."

24

It took a lot of persuading to convince Mum and Dad they'd chosen a sleepover in an abandoned chapel over comfy hotel beds. But like a bad dream, their memories of the last twelve hours get fuzzier the further we go from the Necropolis Railway Station. By the time we arrive back in Greyscar, they've completely rewritten history.

"Wasn't that a lovely weekend?" asks Mum, as we arrive back at our house and funeral parlour on Deadman's Drive.

"I definitely feel like I've had a break from

reality," says Dad, eyeing Rusty's pocket where Fang is curled up asleep. "I can't believe we agreed to buy you *that*."

"Fangor Death Render, Emissary to Karak Zhor, Slaughter Lord of the Seventh Battalion is not a *that*," says Rusty indignantly.

I grin and shake my head at poor Fang's ridiculous full name. It's good to be home.

There's a familiar squawk as we pull onto our driveway and I'm out of the car like a shot.

Phrank is sitting beneath the laurel hedge. He fixes me with two beady orange eyes and shakes his head. It's a judgy kind of look.

I kneel on the grass and peer under the hedge at him. "I'm sorry. If I could have taken you with me, I would have."

Phrank's having none of it and turns his back on me.

It stings like a slap.

I sigh. There's only one thing I can do to win him over, one thing he can't resist: food.

Dad opens the side door and we all troop inside the house. I go straight to the snack cupboard in the kitchen, but Rusty disappears off in the opposite direction, towards the funeral parlour.

"What are you doing?"

"I'll tell you in a minute. Meet you outside."

I grab a packet of sunflower seeds for Phrank and head back into the garden, leaving Mum and Dad to make that cup of tea they've been banging on about for the last hour.

It's a bright October afternoon and after leaving a trail of seeds from the hedge up to the back door, I take a seat on the doorstep. The moment Phrank pokes his head out from beneath the hedge and starts to eat, I know I'm halfway forgiven.

Then Rusty arrives holding Fang, and I swear I see Phrank scowl.

"Phrank meet Fang. Fang meet Phrank," I say.

Rusty puts Fang down and he starts to nibble at the seeds. Phrank gives a warning *cark*.

"Be nice," I warn. "Fang is one of us now."

They eye each other suspiciously, but at least it's not out-and-out war.

"Parent-napping, the fortune-teller from hell and deadly Death Shadows," says Rusty, coming to join me on the step. "Mum's idea of the perfect holiday."

We both crack up, until Phrank and Fang are looking at us like they need to call help. After everything we've been through, it's a relief to finally be able to behave our ages again.

"Okay, enough, enough, I can't breathe," I say.

Rusty turns his face to the sun.

"We did it though. We saved Mum and Dad and that calls for a celebration brownie." He produces a large slab of chocolatey goodness and breaks it in half.

We manage to eat almost all of it without Fang and Phrank stealing any. Which is a result because the thing these two seem to have most in common is a shared love of food.

"Not to put a downer on everything, but what are we going to do now?" asks Rusty.

I pick at the frayed patch on my jeans. "Something happened that night on the beach in that vision I saw. Our Spooksmith ancestor—"

"—Viola," interrupts Rusty. "I went to the funeral parlour to check out the family portraits. It was the only name beginning with V."

"Viola." I roll the name around my mouth.

"You don't suppose, just for once, your Spooksmith powers could have shown you a vision of three kids kicking back and having a fun night out?"

"I wish." I snort. "Look, Hell Mary called our powers 'unnatural' and I'm starting to agree with her."

"That rippling thing was weird, but I'm not sure I'd listen to a control freak with a bloody crystal ball who dresses like Morticia Addams on a bad day."

I shrug. "I just want to know why trouble keeps finding us. We're putting Mum and Dad in danger. We have to take control before something goes really wrong."

"More wrong than visiting the dead side?"

"We've got some more pieces of the puzzle at least. We know that Viola Spooksmith and Malachi Innspectre are two of the sets of initials on the symbol in the crypt. We know that they, along with this mysterious L.W., made a mistake that ruined their lives. I believe the answer is out there. We just have to find it."

"So, we investigate?"

"We investigate."

Rusty produces a thick black notepad and hands it to me.

It's our Spooksmith casebook.

I flick past the Cinderman entry and write: *Hell Mary*. Then we list everything we've learned, from our ghostly defences not working on the other side, to Death Shadows being drawn to fire.

My pen is still hovering above the page when a phone rings somewhere in the house. My muscles twitch.

"It can't be her, can it?"

Rusty laughs and takes the notepad and pen from me. In answer, he writes:

Hell Mary. Departed. Case closed.

And then he slams the book shut.

"Enough Spooksmithing for one weekend," he says. "How about we team up and persuade Mum and Dad to order pizza?"

"Triple cheese?"

Rusty grins. "Now you're talking."

I follow Rusty and Fang and Phrank into the house. We've still got a lot of questions that need answering, but our Spooksmith team is growing and so is our knowledge of dealing with the other side.

Ghostly problems? Bring them on.

TOP SECRET

A Spooksmiths Guide

AKA what we've found out so far...

SPOOKSMITH FACTS

- We're ghost-marked. It looks like a birthmark.

    > Except it's not... The mark means that on our twelfth birthday we got an extra-special present: we could see and hear the dead. We're not Smiths any more. We're Spooksmiths.

- The good news: the mark gives us some protection from evil ghosts.

    > And we get animal sidekicks: Phrank the pheasant and Fang the rat.

- The bad news: the ghost mark skips generations and we don't know anyone else alive who has it.

    > Also, we think our marks are linked to these things called Death Shadows, whose job it is to keep the dead and the living apart. Our ghost marks ripple in their presence.

- There's a ~~crypt~~ *(ghost prison)* underneath our home and parents' business, Serenity Funerals, containing evil ghosts trapped in urns. Entry is through the bookcase.

- *There's a symbol on the crypt wall at home showing three sets of letters, V.S., L.W. and M.I. We now know the letters are initials. V.S. stands for Viola Spooksmith and M.I. stands for Malachi Innspectre. We don't know who L.W. is, but we know all three of them were once friends and made a mistake that ruined their lives.*

We need to find out what they did!

GHOST FACTS

- Ghosts stick around because of unfinished business.

- A ghost's real name has power.
    - (The one they had when they were alive)

- All ghosts have a tether tying them to the living world.
    - The Cinderman's was his heart. Hell Mary had somehow trapped her own reflection in a mirrored necklace.

- Necropolis City is a weird, in-between place for Victorian ghosts. It's patrolled by Death Shadows who keep the dead, the living and ghosts from other timelines apart. Live humans like us are hunted to death.
    - Are there other in-between places for ghosts?

- The journey to Necropolis City is by ghost train. It's run by a spook made of flies called Malachi Innspectre.
    - The Necropolis Railway was a real thing. Look it up...

- The Cinderman had to be defeated by sunset. ← Hell Mary had to be defeated by sunrise.

- Lavender, salt and sage burn ghosts in the real world. But they don't work in Necropolis City!!

- Ghostly powers are rated one to five. Category Ones and Twos are generally weak and friendly, but higher up the spook scale things can get nasty. We're pretty sure Seba was a Category Four because he could make the living hear him. Hell Mary was hands down a Cat Five like the Cinderman.

  She was ultimate evil, but we got her!

  Although he turned out to be all right in the end.

DON'T MISS INDIGO AND RUSTY'S FIRST SPINE-CHILLING ADVENTURE...

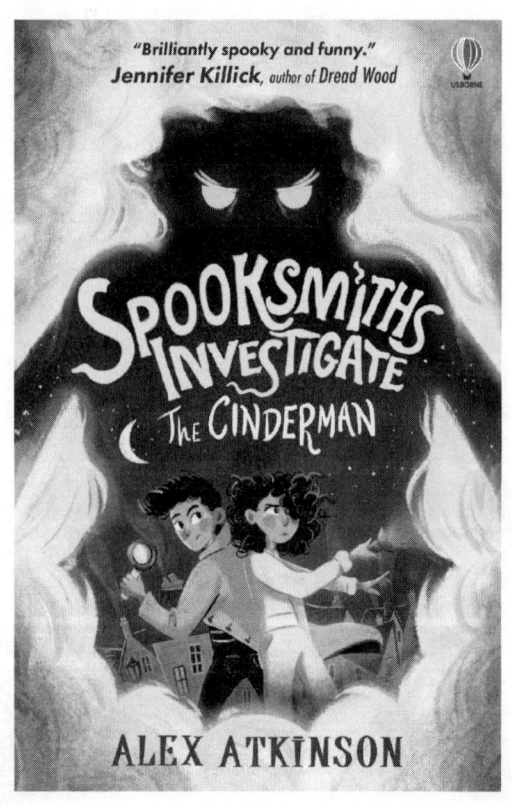

When Indigo drops an old urn, she accidentally releases the Cinderman: a terrifying ash monster, who will smother their town in ashes and turn everyone into zombies, unless they can stop him by sunset.

Using their newly awakened Spooksmith skills, Indigo and Rusty set out to enlist the help of other ghosts. But can the Blasted Banshee and Chuckles the Phantom Toddler really help them find the Cinderman's true name and put him in his grave for good before Ashmageddon strikes?

"Brilliantly spooky and funny."
Jennifer Killick, author of *Dread Wood*

"Spine-chilling terror and laughs on every page."
S.J. Wills, author of *Bite Risk*

ACKNOWLEDGEMENTS

My brilliant agent, Lina Langlee, thank you for finding my darkly funny stories a home and for taking me around Edinburgh to meet so many wonderful booksellers.

Team Usborne, thank you so much for continuing Indigo and Rusty's journey with me. Sarah Stewart, I am so grateful that I get to work with you. Your edits, enthusiasm and support make the whole process a joy. Charlotte James, Hannah Featherstone, Gareth Collinson, Amelia Mehra, Jacob Dow, Fritha Lindqvist and Georgia Allen, thank you for all the expert editorial, marketing and PR support. Sarah Cronin, thank you for the text design, and Kath Millichope and Miriam Serafin, thank you for creating another cracking book cover.

Team family: Mum, Nick, Jen and Phoebe. Thank you for the Hazell sense of humour and the endless support. Miss you, Dad. Peter, Jane, Catherine, Ben, Tom, Harry, Uncle John, Aunty Carol and not forgetting my favourite cousins Mark and Sam and their families, thank you for always being there and for cheering me on.

Bill, Ellie and Edward, you make me believe I can do anything. I'm so lucky to have the three of you in my life.

A huge thank you to everyone who has read and supported Spooksmiths. I've met some truly incredible people over the last year. Big shout out to Blackwell's for making *Spooksmiths Investigate: The Cinderman* the October 2024 Children's Book of the Month and to Mae Gaynor, bookseller at Blackwell's Oxford for championing it. Oodles of thanks to the FCBG and to all the adults and children involved in putting me on the FCBG Children's Book Award 2025 Younger Readers Shortlist.

Extra helpings of appreciation to October Jones at Roehampton Library, Sheryl, Wendy, Louise and the team at Chorleywood Bookshop, Wicki, Matt, Alice and the team at Berkhamsted Waterstones – not forgetting all the amazing teachers, teaching assistants, librarians, booksellers and pupils I've met on library and school visits. Thank you for listening to me waffle on and for voting "rat" when it came to helping me choose Rusty's animal sidekick. Special mention to Isla Doubal: thank you for using your marvellous artistic talents to bring Phrank the pheasant to life for my author assembly.

Fellow writers are the best. Natalia Godsmark and Sarah Frend, you are wonderful writers and critique partners, I couldn't do it without you. Clare Harlow and Emily Randall Jones, both fabulous talents and fabulous human beings. Thank you for answering my many authory questions. Kristina Rahim thank you for the advice and laughs and to Maggie, for sitting through and critiquing my first attempt at a virtual school visit and for being so nice about it. Jennifer Killick and SJ Wills gave lovely quotes for *The Cinderman.* Definite pinch me moments.

Stuart White and all who sail with the good ship WriteMentor, SCBWI, SCBWI UV 2022, Boot Campers 2024, #2024 debut group and the Herts Local Authors group, it's so good to be a part of these communities and chats.

This last year has been a tough one. Thank you to all my friends who've supported me and made me laugh in some of the darkest times. You know who you are, and I couldn't have got through it without you.

My final thank you goes to you, the reader. Thank you for picking up this book. I hope you enjoyed it.

ABOUT THE AUTHOR

Alex Atkinson loves scary books filled with oddball characters. She blames her idyllic North Yorkshire childhood spent playing murder-in-the-dark and listening to her dad's blood-curdling bedtime stories. After studying English and Politics at Newcastle University, she worked as a website content editor. She now lives in a village in Hertfordshire with her husband, kids and dogs, but dreams of abandoned buildings, ghosts and zombies.

SPOOKSMITHS INVESTIGATE is her debut series.